"At last, here is a book that addresses this question about 'Midnight Creeping'. In her unique book, Ms. Hudson explores significant and powerful events that will educate readers on how important it is to sow goods seeds because what goes around comes back around".

Phillip Ganzel, M.D.
Dougherty Pediatrics

~~~

"I was once told as a child, 'what goes on in the dark will come to the light'. That statement is true and the character in this story, Gaylin Harris, opens the door for light to undercover his darkness. This book is highly recommended and I hope that everyone would receive a thoughtful message".

Alice Marie Hayward
Southside Elementary School
Cairo, Georgia

~~~

Reviews

"A well written story authored by a beautiful woman who I adore. This book is Heavenly sent and is much needed for topic of discussion. I truly enjoyed reading every chapter and the ending was superb!"

Greg Croxton Attorney at Law
Croxton Law Group, P.C.
(Phi Beta Sigma Fraternity)

~~~

"Wow! We are honored to have an input on this outstanding novel. First of all, buy the book. Secondly, read the book. Last but not least, feel free to pass the word along because after you all read this book it would be worth sharing. God bless"!

Calvin & Joanna Dennis, Phoebe Putney Memorial Hospital
Cameron Dennis, Phoebe Putney Memorial Hospital
Captain Jennifer L. Dennis, United States Military

~~~

"A true lady of God who has written another great book! Stay true to yourself, sister, and know that all things are possible for ones that believe and allow God to manifest. This novel is highly recommended."

Dr. Curtis A. Hudson Sr.
Ocala Animal Clinic

Midnight Creeping, Early Morning Reaping

Melissa Diane Hudson, M.A.

DragonEye Publishing

Midnight Creeping, Early Morning Reaping
by Melissa Diane Hudson, M.A.
Copyright 2013 Melissa Diane Hudson, M.A.

Edited by Amy Collins

First Edition 2013
First Printing February 2013

ISBN 13: 978-1-61500-025-8 (Paperback)
ISBN 13: 978-1-61500-089-0 (Ebook)
ISBN 13: 978-1-61500-026-5   (Hardback Case Bound)

Library of Congress Control Number: 2012951899

10 9 8 7 6 5 4 3 2 1

Manufactured in the United States of America

Visit our website
www.DragonEyePublishers.com
Orders@DragonEyePublishers.com

Published by
DragonEye Publishing
753A Linden Place
Elmira, NY 14901 USA

DEDICATIONS

In loving memory of my loving husband and mother

My husband:
Dr. Curtis Hudson Jr.
Sunrise- December 26, 1970 Sunset- December 31, 2010

My mother:
Linda L. Willis- Dennis
Sunrise- June 23, 1955 Sunset- June 13, 1984

Living in Heaven is better than living on earth. I will always love you all.

Acknowledgments

First and foremost, I acknowledge God who is the head of my life. I thank Him for allowing me to do His will and who has been there for me through the good times and the bad. God is my source that has blessed me tremendously. To everyone out there that does not believe in dreams and miracles, think twice, have faith, and a little patience, and God will be to your rescue if only you give Him your life.

I would like to thank my late husband, Dr. Curtis Hudson Jr., for his love, input, and patience through this novel's creation. I thank him for allowing me to turn one of our bedrooms into an office so that I could create more inspirational stories that seek to make a difference. I am eternally thankful for God had sent me such a wonderful spouse.

I also would like to thank my son, Curtis Hudson III, for being such an awesome toddler who appreciates my time when I am dutifully fulfilling the will of God.

My two siblings thank you for your kind support. To everyone who has been very supportive, your good deeds will never go unnoticed.

For all the readers who will purchase a copy of this book, I truly thank you in advance and hope that you receive a thoughtful message and blessing that will impact and empower your life forever. Feel free to pass the word along. Be Blessed!

"You have heard the Law of Moses says, "Do not commit adultery. But I say, anyone who even looks at a woman with lust in his eye has already committed adultery with her in his heart. So if your eye- even if it is your good eye-causes you to lust, gouge it out and throw it away. It is better for you to lose one part of your body than for your whole body to be thrown into hell." --Matthew 5:27-37

TABLE OF CONTENTS

Foreword

I thank and praise God for allowing Melissa Diane Hudson's book to be published. "Diane", is what I call her, is very talented and creative when it comes to writing Christian literature. When she first mentioned this title *Midnight Creeping, Early Morning Reaping,* I knew that the story would serve its purpose. The book was written to sound a call to all adulterers and cheaters that what they do in the dark might not bring them back to the light.

They say, "Hell hath no fury like a woman scorned, and vengeance is bitter sweet". Women are now becoming the perpetrators in domestic violence cases and are taking the laws into their own hands when it comes to seeking the ultimate revenge against a cheating spouse or lover. Some women are fed up with men stepping on them like doormats and treating them like "fools". *Midnight Creeping, Early Morning Reaping* indicates how a psychopathic scorned woman takes "sweet revenge" to a whole new level.

Many men say with their mouth that they want a good woman to marry and bear kids with her, but then when God blesses him with that great wife and mother to his kids, then he wants to "play the field" or chase behind another dress tail and think that the grass is greener on the other side. In fact, from a distance, the grass may appear greener or prettier. But in actuality, the grass is not greener and it must be watered just like the other. Sometimes the most beautiful things that attract human nature are the ones we cannot or should not have. That is what gets a lot of people in trouble. They desire shiny and nice things and would pay a hefty price to satisfy the lust of the flesh.

Melissa Diane Hudson's book, *Midnight Creeping, Early Morning Reaping* uncovers events in the story that explains what may have triggered a once faithful husband into a cheater. Adultery is wrong and is one of the Ten Commandments. It's like the old saying, "You reap what you sow". Therefore, sow good seeds on good grounds and watch God bring forth a great harvest.

Darlene Bevins
Middle School Teacher,
Tax Associate

Introduction:
Midnight Creeping, Early Morning Reaping

Midnight creeping sometime brings upon early morning weeping.

Why? Because the villain in this story, Gaylin Harris, receives more than what he bargains for when he decides to cheat on his Christian, paralyzed wife, Gail, with scandalous women.

Gaylin Harris is evil, more poisonous than the venom in a snake. He plays malicious mind games with his wife's emotions and uses her handicap as a cruel way to enslave her mentality so that she will remain a prisoner behind closed doors.

With countless years of infidelity, he finally meets "lips of death" Loretta Cox, who is beautiful, sexy, and dazzling-everything he hopes to find in a mistress, but she is a psychopathic deranged outcast who takes "sweet revenge" to a whole new level that spurs her into one of the world's most dramatic, bloodthirsty rampages. What is known as a game to Gaylin has now become a vicious cycle. No one knows how the game will end, but after everything is said and done, he will reap what he sowed.

Midnight Creeping, Early Morning Reaping, sounds a call to all cheaters that what they do in the dark, may not bring them back to the light.

Part 1

Seeing the Whole Picture

One:
Warning Comes Before Destruction

It's Friday night, and the bedroom is candle lit with the sweet scent of Honey Breeze air freshener wafting around the house. The room's warm atmosphere gives it an inviting ambiance. Gory Rob's soft soulful song "Tonight Is the Night" is sounding from the radio. Two nearly full wine glasses sit on the end table next to a Bible as a half-dressed beautiful woman walks seductively into the bedroom, carrying a red rose in her hand. She politely hands the rose to Gaylin, who lies across the full-sized bed admiring her irresistible beauty. The lady slowly crawls on top of him and passionately kisses him as if it is his last. Arousal heats his body as drips of sweat fall down his face.

She instantly pulls out a long white cord from inside her black briefcase and ties his hands tightly to the bedposts. She blindfolds his eyes with a white cotton handkerchief as she reaches over on the end table and takes a sip of red wine. She evilly laughs like the devil in disguise, while stroking his muscular body with her long fingertips.

Rage suddenly bellowed from within as a quick glimpse from her past crept into her mind. She pulls out a box cutter from underneath the bed and aggressively slashes him across the face and neck. *Punishment for sin may be swift and severe. Punishment is a consequence of sinful action,* she thinks as blood gushes violently onto the silky red sheets. Anguish cries linger outside through the night air, leaving a trail of echoes.

Twenty-eight years earlier, On September 30, 1980, Gail Bradford and Gaylin Harris prepare to unite in Holy

Matrimony at the cathedral in Miami, Florida. She has that special love for him that flows deeply through the veins, capturing segments of cells that hold so much passion. Her family and friends told her that this man was too good to be true. He was very dangerous, vindictive and just as evil as Satan himself.

"Hello, honey. How are things coming along with the wedding?" Gail's mother said, while walking in the house with a handful of grocery bags.

Gail looked in amazement before speaking.

"Oh, I've been running around trying to have everything perfect for my big day. I want everything to look awesome."

"I still think it's a bad idea to get married. Sugar, you know nothing about this boy."

"Mother, please. All I need to know that he loves me."

"Love? Since when have that boy showed you any love? He's always talking about himself and speaks badly of women. Baby, if a man can't respect another woman, then what makes you think he will respect you?" Gail's mother said, as she places the canned goods into the food pantry, one by one.

"Mother, enough about my man, try to keep your comments to yourself because I don't want Gaylin to get the wrong impression about you, got it?" She said while standing in the kitchen flipping the pages of a 1980 *African American Magazine*.

Gail is just the typical nice girl next door who Mother Nature skipped over when beauty was being passed around. Although she doesn't have the face of a queen, she possesses an everlasting Godly spirit that manifests on the inside that makes her more worthy than anyone with physical beauty. Mrs. Bradford, her mother, models her life by the Bible and only wants what's best for her daughter.

The two keep conversing about the upcoming wedding as they are interrupted by the sound of a horn blowing in the front yard. Gail peeps out the door and notices a 1974 Red Mustang parked in the driveway. A pretty woman strutting her hips in a black spaghetti dress switches as she walks near the house in her three-inch heel pumps.

"Monice!" Gail yells in excitement while standing on the front porch wearing a raggedy white apron. "Wow, you look like you've stepped out of a fashion magazine! Girl, those bony leg runway models don't have anything on you. Come on in and make yourself at home."

Monice warmly smiles as the glitter in her lip-gloss sparkles.

"Girl, I don't half-step when it comes to me looking good. You never know whom you might run into."

Gail agrees, while escorting the lady into the kitchen to meet her mother, who is sitting in a wobbly, old worn down chair at the breakfast table eating a slice of pound cake and drinking a glass of cold milk.

"So, you're going through with this wedding? Girl, my cousin has never settled down with one woman. One lady is not enough for his bedroom. He likes them all: white, black, Hispanic, Asian, you name it. He doesn't discriminate," Monice sarcastically said.

Every time Monice takes a look in the mirror, it was like looking at her cousin Gaylin with long wavy hair. From their hazel-brown eyes, jet-black hair and cinnamon smooth skin that were inherited from a mixed blend of African and Indonesian heritage, it was obvious that they shared the same bloodline.

"Watch your filthy mouth, child. I don't allow that kind of ungodly talk in here," Mrs. Bradford said as she eases out of the worn down chair in the kitchen and walks back into the living room and turns on the television.

Gail takes a deep breath before speaking.

"I get so sick and tired of people trying to rule my life. Back off, will you?"

"Girl, I'm just trying to help your butt out. I know my cousin. You're not his type, anyway. You're too churchy. He likes girls that wear the tight skimpy clothes, long wigs all down their backs, heavy makeup, and, yeah, the big butt," Monice said as she slaps herself on the behind.

"Talking about the kind that looks like you?" Dion bitterly said while walking in the house from the front door. "Don't take it personal. I'm just showing Gail a cheap sample of what her fiancé might like."

"I beg your pardon?"

"Oh, did I step on your toes? Excuse me. They always said a hit dog will holler," Dion said as she plops down on the sofa next to Mrs. Bradford, who is deeply engaging in a television show.

"So you got jokes, huh?" Monice said. "You wish you had this big nice butt."

"Stop all the bickering. This is a special time in my life and I want everyone to get along."

Dion is Gail's best friend who hates the idea that she is planning to marry a senseless, egotistical womanizer that despises the ground she walks on. Early the next morning around nine o'clock, the telephone rings several times before Gail retrieves it. She wobbles over to the table and quickly answers and discovers that it is Gaylin, happily calling from Connecticut.

"Honey, I got the job. I finally got my big break as a star actor. The producers took one look at my monologue and loved it. We're moving on up like Weezie and George."

"I am so proud of you. How much will you be making?" Gail asked with the telephone to her ear.

"Baby, I will be paid top dollars. I don't know the exact figures yet. But I heard that the pay is great," he said in excitement. "I'm on my way, now."

"That's great, honey. So have you thought about the wedding that will be going on in two weeks?"

"Huh? What wedding? No one told me about a wedding."

Gail's eyes got big, "our wedding, stupid! Don't tell me that you've been so busy that you forgot!"

"Oh yeah, that wedding," he remembered. "There's no need to rush things. We have all the time in the world. I have enough things on my plate to deal with."

"Enough things on your plate to deal with?" She angrily snapped. "What could be more important than you being a father to your child? Before you got this job you said that we were going to be married! I've been here running around stiff big trying to make arrangements for our big day!"

"We will get married one day, but today is not the time to talk about it. I'm just getting started in my career and I need to stay focused," Gaylin said, seriously. "Frankly, I have big plans that don't quite include a wife and a baby, maybe one day when I'm thirty."

"You chose one helluva time to tell me that you're not ready for marriage! Don't try to get out of this one! I didn't get pregnant by myself! I had big plans, too! I wanted to attend college and do something good with my life! Listen, you're not even worth a hand in marriage! Lose my number you son of a ___!" *Click.* Gail slams down the telephone and runs heartbrokenly to her bedroom.

Laying face up in her bed starring straight at the ceiling, Gail's heart sank. She remembered a few months ago in high school stepping across the lawns of Burger Land, racing to the parking lot to meet Gaylin, who was sitting in the front seat of his friend's Chevrolet. That was the very first day he expressed his love for her and she soon after gave him her virginity. She wished she didn't have to think about it all as if it just happened. It was just a brief period in her life she hoped would disappear.

"Wake up lazy bone!" Dion interrupts Gail's train of thoughts as she shouts, while strutting over in a very happy mood flashing all white teeth.

"I'm not sleep."

"Girl, why are you still in your nightgown? We have a ten o'clock appointment this morning with the florist about your wedding flowers."

"Wedding? There's not going to be one," Gail murmured as she stuffs her head in the pillow.

"Girl, that's the best thing you've said all day. Don't worry, you're better off without that scum bag," Dion said in laughter. "He doesn't deserve you."

Gail has tears and pain in her eyes as she thinks about her ungrateful fiancé, who is in Connecticut hanging around celebrities and high maintenance music performers.

"Gail, you will not stay in this house and sulk all day." Dion grabs the pillow off Gail's face. "Go and get dressed and have some fun. Stop wasting your time thinking about Gaylin. He's not thinking about you."

"I love him. Maybe he needs time to think about all of this. He needs time to think about me and the baby."

"Gail, wake up and smell the coffee. Guys like Gaylin only think about himself," Dion said in her usual serious tone. "It's not the end of the world. Forget about him and go out and find you a real man, someone who is going to treat you right."

"Listen to you. You're sounding like my mother. I love him. I'm carrying his child." She rubs her belly.

"So what? It's the eighties. A lot of women carry men's babies and not get married. Just join the crowd like everyone else."

"Are you deranged, or plan out stupid? I'm not going to have a bastard baby walking around here without a father," Gail said in frustration, as she turns her attention away from Dion, who is still staring at her with both hands on her hips.

"You should of thought about that before you had sex. I'm quite sure your pastor preaches about fornication. If you didn't want to get pregnant out of wedlock, then you shouldn't have given up the goods before the honeymoon."

"Yeah, I know I made a huge mistake. That's why I want to do things right, by getting married," she said. "I know he would make a great father."

"You need to seriously think about what you're doing. Marriage is nothing to play with. Once you make those vows before God, then death is the only separation. Unless that fool starts beating the crap out of you, or you catch him cheating with some woman," Dion jokingly said while laughing.

While Gail and Dion continue to argue about her future commitment to Gaylin, the telephone rings and it is Monice on the line, demanding her for Gaylin's personal telephone number.

"I need my cousin's direct number," Monice said rudely, without greeting Gail with a hello. "I tried calling the office, but I haven't received an answer. I keep getting a busy signal."

The vein in Gail's forehead bulged, as she swallowed hard.

"I don't give away Gaylin's personal telephone number. Maybe he'll give it to you himself."

"What? This is important. I need to speak to my cousin."

"I'm sorry, Monice, but I—"

"Alright!" She cuts Gail off. "I'll get it some other time! You have a good day!" *Click.* She hangs up the telephone.

"See there. That heifer is trouble. I'm warning you Gail to not get involved with that family. Those people might be crazy," Dion said, giving her hair a toss. "I've heard about cases like that in the big city."

"Dion, that's enough! Gaylin this, Gaylin that! I'm tired of the whole thing! Just go and leave me *be!* I got too much stress as it is!" she roared as she left the room with the door slightly ajar.

Later that afternoon around four o'clock, Gail notices from the front porch the mail carrier placing a red envelope into the mailbox right before he drives to the next house in his muddied white mail jeep. She joyfully runs to the mailbox as if she knows that the letter is from Gaylin, who she still loves and adores. While ripping open the neatly folded letter, her heart fiercely beats with anxiety as the sweat slowly drips from her face.

The note is printed in bold letters asking Gail to meet Gaylin in Connecticut on May 27th, the day of their wedding. After reading the note, Gail immediately feels very nervous and sick to her stomach, and a tear falls down from her eye, because now she knows definitely that there will not be a wedding. So, she walks spiritlessly back into the house and curls up onto the sofa.

On May 27th, Gail prepares herself to aboard the next airline to Stanford, Connecticut. She sits beside an elderly couple on the plane and wishes that it were herself and Gaylin. She looks at the couple and starts a simple conversation.

"Oh, you all look so lovely. How many years have you all been married?"

"We have been married for almost seventy- five years. Our wedding anniversary is tomorrow," The elderly lady said with a sparkle in her eye.

Gail's face beams with admiration as she watches the happy couple.

"How did you do it? How can someone stay married that long with all this temptation out there?" she asked, desperately wanting to know the answer.

"You have to have God in it and to be with the right person. Without God, Satan can ruin a marriage in a heartbeat," the man answered, seriously staring into her brown eyes. "Don't become an unequal yolk."

"What if your mate doesn't want to serve God, and he is only concerned with materialistic things and his career?" She sadly uttered to the couple that leans closer to her seat.

"Well, honey, don't marry the joker," the man firmly stated. "Don't put yourself in a bad situation before it happens. If you already know that this fellow is bad news, then don't think that he will change once you are married. Honey, you'll be like Humpty Dumpty, setting yourself up for a very big fall. Me and my wife have been married for almost seventy-five years and have had only one big argument."

"Really! How did you all manage to get along for all those years?" Gail questioned with surprise as she moved closer to the couple.

"We're still trying to end that argument," the pair said in laughter, as the pilot announces that the next stop would be in New York.

The plane has arrived and the airport was more crowded than Gail anticipated. The walkways were filled with business and everyday looking people carrying luggage and talking on pay phones. She retrieves her luggage and passes the ticket booth and searches around for Gaylin, but he isn't there. She waits for several hours until she decides to take the next cab to the address in Connecticut, where he is temporary residing.

Gail's cab pulled up in front of the apartment building. She paid the driver and then gathered her belongings. However, when she arrives at the apartment, she sees with surprise his car is at home. She goes inside the lobby and takes the elevator to his apartment. Gail yells his name as she knocks forcefully on the door. But when Gaylin peeps through the peephole and notices his fiancée, he bangs his hand in anger against the door. He adjusts the towel around his nude body and turns on the light. Her smile fades as he opens the door; Gail receives the biggest greeting that brought tears to her eyes.

Two:
Look Deep Before You Leap

"Gaylin, I had no idea! I had no idea that you would do this!" She cried as she runs inside the apartment, knocking over packed boxes that were sitting on the floor near the door.

Gaylin had lit vanilla-scented candles and made a path of red rose petals leading to the bedroom with a sign posted over the doorway stating *will you marry me today*?

"You kind of caught me off guard. I wanted everything to have been a surprise. I thought I told you to call me once your plane landed." He turned towards Gail.

"Oh my, everything looks so beautiful." Gail ignored the statement while looking around admiring the beautiful decorations. Why did you ask me to come here?"

"Baby, I asked you to come here today because I want us to be together forever. I was thinking about our last conversation and decided to stop putting things before you. I want to be a father to my child," Gaylin said as he takes Gail's luggage.

"But why were you being so negative over the telephone? I thought you didn't want to marry me."

"Ssshhh," he whispered in her ear as he places a soft sensuous kiss on her cheek.

"It was just my ego talking, sweetheart," he sincerely said. "I love you and our unborn child. You are a good woman. Every man needs a good woman to stand behind him."

"No, baby, a good woman stands beside her man, and that's what I intend to do," Gail said while holding his hand.

The two stare at one another with huge smiles upon their face. Gaylin kisses her hand and says, "I'm glad that you're here. I want to make you very happy. But in the meantime, I have something very special for you hanging up in the bedroom. Let me cover your beautiful eyes and escort you."

But before he could open the door, Gail passionately embraces him, releasing a lustful feeling of desire. They walk into the bedroom, bed covered with rose petals with an extra-large silk nightie lying next to a cotton-filled pillow. Gaylin gently lays his fiancée on the bed and massages her pregnant belly.

"You're the greatest. Every moment I spend with you it makes me feel so special," she said, while running her fingers through his soft, wavy black hair.

"Baby, for now on, you shouldn't listen to those hostile girls who don't have a man. They just jealous and want what you have. I'm a hardworking good man and everyone knows it," he arrogantly said, flashing all perfect white teeth.

"Yeah, I owe you an apology for not trusting in our love for one another. I allowed my mother, family and friends to interfere. Sweetie, it won't happen again, Gail said with sincerity.

"I'm not like the other brothers out there that are just trying to get a quick fix. I don't play games or run from commitment. I stand up for what's mine and take on responsibilities. Enough about this, do you accept my proposal?" he said while bending down on one knee.

"Yes, with every breath in me, Gaylin, you know how I feel about you."

"Well, alright then. It's time to celebrate. Gail, I'm taking you out tonight to one of the finest nightclubs in Connecticut. "

"Gaylin, honey, you know how I hate clubs. I've never been the partying type."

"So what? You're going to be married to a very famous man. You better get used to going out to jazzy nightclubs and dining at exquisite restaurants and meeting classy people, who have made it to the top. Unlike the losers you know back home who're still counting nickels and pennies out of a jelly jar. Baby, we're hanging with the big dogs. People who own a bunch of land, houses, banks and have stock investments," Gaylin said, as he jumps from off the bed, acting macho by parading around with his chin held high.

"What's inside a person's wallet doesn't determine who they are inside. Gaylin, I know some of the nicest people who care less about being rich and hanging out with the end crowd. Frankly, I would rather be with some down to earth people who know how to love and treat one another, people who live by the Bible."

"See, that's what wrong with this world today! Small-minded folks like you would rather settle and continue to be a doormat under the rich man's feet! That's why some people can't get ahead in life because they're so stuck on stupid! I thought you were different! You're no different than your country butt mama!" Gaylin shouted while grabbing an outfit from his closet and marches into the bathroom and slams the door shut. Gail gloomily sits up on the side of the bed with her head held downward.

"Why are you just sitting there looking stupid?" Gaylin opened the bathroom door and yelled out to her. "Go get dressed! I don't have all night to be bothered with you!"

"Honey, I want to take a shower first. It's been a long day," she said with a crack in her voice.

He comes out of the bathroom and fumbles into his linen cabinet for a towel and a bar of soap. "Go in the kitchen and wash up," he said as he throws the towel and bar of soap to her. "I don't have time for you to stay all night in the bathroom using up all my hot water. I have some important people who will be meeting us tonight and I'm not going to be late."

"But, Gaylin. I need to take a bath in the bathtub. I'm pregnant. I don't feel comfortable washing off in a sink. It'll only take a few minutes for me to run some warm water," she said nervously, holding the towel that he threw at her.

"Woman, are you hard of hearing!" He shouted, standing in the bedroom bare chest with water dripping off his Carmel muscular body. "Get your fat butt dressed and make it snappy! I invited Don Wilson and Michael Barron, the executive producers of the million-dollar movie called *Foxed* to be at our engagement dinner! Now you have about ten minutes to bathe your stank behind and comb your nappy-headed hair, because we're almost running late!"

Gail sadly walks back into the living room with her head held down and searches through her luggage for an outfit to wear. She slowly picks up the soap from off the floor and paces over to the kitchen sink to take a quick bath like a scorned child. She later hears Gaylin in the shower, singing along with the radio.

When Gaylin comes out the bathroom he has an annoyed look on his face as he rushes to put on a pair of iron-crisp brown slacks that still had the price tag attached to the belt loop. Gail was in the bedroom mirror, primping and applying makeup. They heard a slight knock on the front door.

Knock. Knock!

"Who is it?" Gaylin asked apprehensively, walking towards the front door.

"Your limo is outside, sir," The limo driver said from the closed door. "Every minute late, is a dollar earned."

"Okay, we'll be right down, just give us a second!" Gaylin shouted to the closed door.

"Woman, are you done yet?" He asked her, while walking into the bedroom where she is prancing around in a green striped colored dress, smiling from ear to ear.

"Yeah, baby. I'm almost done. How do I look?" She happily said, spinning around the room like a princes. "I wanted to surprise you in it."

"Yeah. I'm surprised. Now, take that Halloween costume off before you make a fool of me. I'm not going to look like an idiot in front of these important people."

"Baby, Mama spent good money on this outfit. It's quite appropriate for the event."

"Don't fat mouth me, woman! I said take that cheap looking dress off and if I have to tell you again, I'm going upside your head with my fist!" He snapped angrily, frowning at her with a balled fist.

Twenty minutes later, Gaylin and Gail walk downstairs of his upscale apartment, located downtown, where mostly all the rich reside. Gail is walking slowly in a two-inch matching pumps, checking her makeup in a compact mirror. The limo driver opens the door for the couple and then drives them to Club Paris Persian, which is only a few blocks from Gaylin's apartment.

When they arrived, people were waiting in line looking elegant in fancy dresses and business suits. Club Paris Persian was popular for attracting famous Oscar winning movie stars like Hank Mathews, Tina Garget, Goldie Richie, Millisa Van Wison and Olivia Rae Hutson. Gaylin and Gail get out of the limo and strut by the crowd, flashing all white teeth. When Gaylin approaches the two bouncers who were standing at the front entrance checking ID from the fake wannabe pop stars, Gaylin signals and the bouncers escort them in the VIP section of the club. Gail walks in nervously, staring around at the crowd who are engaging into personal conversations at their table and at the bar.

"Hello, Mr. Harris. I thought you would never make it," a man dressed in a black suit said to Gaylin before he takes a seat.

"Well, hello, Mr. Wilson and Mr. Barron, this is my beautiful fiancée Gail Bradford," he said, while properly altering his voice.

"Glad to meet you. You are lovelier in person," Mr. Barron said, as he extends his hand to Gail in greeting.

"It's an honor to meet you, too, sir. I've heard awful lot of talk about you."

"Really? Well, I hope it's good. Have a seat you two." The man eagerly said.

Gaylin and Gail sit at the table with the two men and engage in conversation.

"Would you all like a drink?" Mr. Wilson asked, as he sips on a glass of wine.

"Oh, no. I don't drink that stuff. Good old ice water with a lemon would do me just fine," Gail said, looking serious.

The two men glance at each other with a smirk on their face. Gaylin becomes embarrass. *Stupid fool*, he thought before reiterating the question.

"Would we like a drink? Sure, what she means is that she's pregnant and doesn't want to hurt the baby, but a small glass won't hurt anything. Right, baby?" He said to her with a forced smile.

"Gaylin, you know that's not true. I don't drink alcohol unless it's the wine that is given during Holy Communion at church."

"Woman, order the wine—"

"Its okay, Gaylin," Mr. Wilson cuts him off. "I understand if she doesn't want to drink. My wife was the same way when she was pregnant."

Mr. Wilson gets up from the table and walks to the bar to get their beverage. Gaylin become silent and tense.

The man arrives back to the table and hands Gail a glass of water and Gaylin a glass of wine. Mr. Barron takes a sip of his wine before speaking.

"So, Mr. Harris, how does it feel to be casted in one of Hollywood's most dramatic movies?"

"Sir, if you only knew. I feel like a million bucks. I've waited on this opportunity since I was a little boy," Gaylin happily said, while smiling at Gail.

"Well, you know this line of business is not an easy task. You must be dedicated and work your fingers to the bone if you ever want to reach Oscar money. But, it does attract attention if you're the type that loves a great audience," Mr. Barron said.

"Attention? Sir, I get that all the time. Someone is always running up to me asking for an autograph or picture," He said, flashing a warm smile while sipping on his glass of wine.

The man pauses, looks at Gaylin straight in the face before laughing.

"That's good. That means you're on your way, young fellow. Keep up the good work. I'd like to propose a toast to your upcoming marriage," Mr. Barron said, while raising his glass. "To this lovely couple, I wish you all the best of luck."
"Amen," Gail said as everyone taps glasses.

A beautiful, young black lady wearing a red strapless dress who has flawless dark skin, the color of a milk chocolate candy bar, interrupts their conversation by elegantly walking over to the table holding a Polaroid camera. Gaylin almost chokes on his drink when he sees the nicely toned lady standing in front of him holding a camera. *Wow!* He lustfully thought.

"Excuse, me, Mr. Harris, can I have a picture with you? I'm your biggest fan." She speaks with great diction.

"Sure." Gaylin sat down his drink and posed with the beautiful lady. Gail looks away in jealousy.

"Oh, silly me, I need for someone to take the picture," the woman said shyly, giggling like an inexperienced high school girl on a first date.

"No problem. My future wife will take the picture. She's not doing nothing but taking up space," Gaylin sarcastically said, holding the young lady around her small waistline.

Gail embarrassingly gets out of her seat and takes the picture. The photo slides out the camera's dispenser. The young lady then gives Gaylin a slight kiss on the cheek before walking away, admiring the beautiful picture.

"See. I told you. This business is always flooded with gorgeous women always throwing themselves at famous celebrities. Mrs. Bradford, just keep an open mind and don't let the stereotype of Hollywood ruin your upcoming marriage," Mr. Wilson said, shaking his glass of wine at her.

"Oh, I'm not worried. I have God watching out for me. God is my way maker."

The two men look at one another with a slight smirk. Gaylin intervened, very frustrated with one leg propped over the other.

"Baby, stop talking about God and the church so much, we're not here to discuss what God has done or will do for you," he said in frustration as he sips on his wine.

"No, Gaylin. I will not stop talking about the Lord. I'm not going to put on a phony face in front of your friends."

Mr. Barron clears his throat before speaking.

"Wow. You are certainly different. If Hollywood thought like you with your morals and values, it wouldn't be Hollywood, it would be Holy-wood," the man laughed, as he takes another sip of wine.

"Yeah. Holy-wood is right. The Christian film market one day is going to take over that place, and I'm going to be the first one there, sitting back in my rocking chair, watching great people like Benny Fusel, Lola Danpress, Renaldo Wilcox and especially Nell Trevande, take the place of all those Satan superstars who are out there posing nude on the screen, just to satisfy this crooked world of sinners."

"Whoa, too much for me! Well, I guess we can prepare to leave. I have a long flight in the morning," Mr. Barron said after making eye contact with Mr. Wilson. "It's been a pleasure meeting you Gail, and Gaylin, keep up the good work." The two men gulp down their wine and get up from the table.

Gail was feeling very uneasy as she walked up the stairs to the apartment. Gaylin walked fast in front of her, filled with anger and rage. When the door swung open, he shoved Gail into the apartment as if she were a ragged doll.

"Who the heck you think you are, embarrassing me like that?" He snapped, pushing her hard against the concrete wall.

"Ahh!" She said in pain, trying to pace her way into the bedroom as she holds her pregnant belly.

"Answer me, woman! The only reason I'm marrying your dumb butt because you're pregnant! I should have never bet that guy in history class those twenty dollars that I'll get you in bed! A big mistake I'll always regret!" He hollered, looking at her with a balled fist.

"A bet! You made a bet that you could get me in bed?" She said with eyes full of water.

"You darn right I did! You church freaks try to act all holier-than-thou, with your long dresses to your feet! You all be the biggest hypocrites, just sitting in back of the church trying to get your groove on! That's why I stopped going to church!"

"I dare you speak to me like this! True, I made one big mistake, but I am darn if I stand here and let you speak down on my love for Christ! Here, take this raggedy behind ring and shove it up your no good butt because I've about had enough for one night!"

Gail angrily storms out of the apartment, leaving luggage and all. Gaylin in a heated rage runs behind her, yelling cruel and hurtful words.

"You can go! I don't need your spotted face, ugly-looking self! I'm famous! I can get me a white or a light-skinned woman! Go on back to the ghetto with your stupid crazy folks and raise that baby by yourself, because you're not getting one red cent from me!" He said with his gruff voice.

Gail races in front of oncoming traffic before flagging down a yellow cab. She jumps in the back seat, very misty eyed.

Three:
Love Got a Hold on Me

Miami was the last place on earth Gail wanted to be besides Connecticut, where the love of her life turned out to be everything that her family and friends had suspected. She tried not to think along those lines because she still had genuine affection for him. When she arrived home, drenched in sweat with dried tear crust on her face, her mother was in the kitchen cooking breakfast. Gail could smell the mouth-watering aroma of turkey bacon, cinnamon pancakes, fried onions and bell pepper as she opens the unlock door.

"Good morning, baby. You're home so early. How was your trip?"

"Oh. It was fine," Gail unhappily said. "What's for breakfast? I'm so hungry, until I could eat a cow." She walks into the kitchen and pours herself a glass of orange juice that is sitting on the table.

"Girl, what's gotten into you? Only last week you were talking about cutting back, eating only fruits and vegetables, trying to stay healthy for the baby."

"What's for breakfast I'm starving?" She ignored the question, as she walks to the stove and sniffs the aroma rising up from the turkey bacon that is frying in the pan.

"Child, get away from that hot grease before you burn yourself. Sit down and tell me all about your trip to the big city." Mrs. Bradford takes a seat in the wobbly chair, smacking on a cooked bacon strip.

Gail wipes the morning crust out of her eyes with her fingertips. She was beginning to feel nauseated as the disturbing words that Gaylin had spoken earlier kept lingering in her mind.

"Girl, are you alright?"

"Yes, Mama, I'm just feeling a little weak that's all. Maybe when I finish eating this good breakfast I'll feel much better."

"Baby, you don't look so good. Let me fix you a plate before you fall out in here." Mrs. Bradford eases out of the chair and attempts to walk over to the stove before she heard Gail run halfway down the hallway, releasing her stomach intakes on the floor. Tears fell down her face. Tears so intense, that she thought she would lose the baby if more fell from her eyes.

"Girl, you need to go see a doctor," Her mother said from the bathroom, running warm water over a washcloth.

"No. I'm alright. I just need to eat."

"Baby, what have you so upset? I can see that something is bothering you," the mother said as she washes Gail's face with the warm cloth.

Gail didn't feel like talking. She became overwhelmed with grief and exhaustion. She got up off the floor and walked into the bathroom and stared at herself in the mirror. Baggy puffy red eyes, smeared lipstick and streaks of brown makeup on her blouse, all accompanied her depressed mood. Her beautiful soft candy curls turned into a nappy Afro. She stared blankly at the unhappy woman in the mirror until the ringing of the telephone interrupted her thoughts.

"Praise the Lord, Bradford residence," the mother joyfully said into the telephone.

"Put Gail on the phone."

"I beg your pardon? Who is this?"

"This is Gaylin, now will you get Gail?" He said rudely.

"Listen, son. Now, I didn't sleep with you on last night so there is no need to call my house with a funky attitude. If you would like to speak to my daughter, I advise you to call back when you get some sense." *Click.* She hangs up the telephone.

"Mama, what did you do? That was Gaylin!" she shouted angrily, running to the telephone and attempts to pick it up. "You had no right to hang up on him!"

"I had all the right! That no good city slicker thinks he can call my house and disrespect me! Oh no! I'm not the one to take mess from a man and I thought I raised you that way, too!" Mrs. Bradford said, shaking a finger at her.

"That's beside the point! You still had no right to hang up on him!"

"You got one helluva mouth on you, girl! That boy is no good! He looks just like the devil himself with those sneaky colored eyes! I don't trust him!" The mother said, very seriously.

"I dare you speak like this about my child's father! Look, you let Daddy slip away right into another woman's arms and now you're trying to ruin my life!" Gail cruelly said. "I don't want to grow old and lonely like you sitting up in this ugly, faded- looking house watching old television sitcoms! I want better! I see why Daddy ran off and left you!"

For a brief moment, there was silence in the room. Mrs. Bradford dolefully lowers her head and slowly walks out onto the front porch. Gail follows behind her, feeling quite ashamed.

"Mama, I'm sorry. I didn't mean to disrespect you." She places her arms around her mother's neck.

"It's okay, baby. Mrs. Bradford speaks softly. "I may not live in a big, fine mansion, but my house is paid off and I keep it clean. Now, that may not be much to you, but it sure was good enough for the four generations that lived here, and I'm proud to sleep in it every night with God and his angels' protection."

"Mama, I didn't mean it that way."

"Hush, child, no need to explain. I do need to mind my own business and keep my big mouth shut when it comes to your love life. I just don't want to see you hurt or taken advantage of. Sweetheart, this is a cold and cruel world and people are doing some crazy stuff. Just promise me that whatever you do you'll include the Lord because He is the only one that will always be around," Mrs. Bradford said, promising to let her daughter live her own life regardless of the consequences.

Days quickly turned into weeks since Gail last heard from Gaylin. She spends her time reading romance fictional novels and fantasizing about her upcoming marriage. She still holds that thought of her and Gaylin becoming husband and wife, despite what everyone else thinks. All that extra daydreaming paid off, because by the end of August, Gaylin had returned to Miami and reunited with Gail.

"What's this about you marrying Gaylin? I thought he had squashed that idea when you ran out on him in Connecticut," Monice said, barging through the unlocked front door unannounced.

"Oh, Monice, I didn't hear you come in," she said, rising sluggishly off the sofa to allow the lady to have a seat. "Yes, we decided to have a private ceremony at the cathedral downtown, just me, my man and the preacher. Boy, I can't wait."

"Private ceremony? Is that right? I think this whole thing is a bunch of nonsense! You need to admit to yourself that my cousin is only marrying you because you're stiff big. If it wasn't for the baby, you would be history, and I--"

"Wait one cotton picking minute!" Gail cuts her off. "Don't come in here trying to tell me what to do! I'm a grown behind woman who is sick and tired of nosy suckers like you all up in my business! Get a life and stay the heck out of mine!"

Gail storms angrily into the bedroom and forcefully slams the wooden door, and knocks down hanging pictures off the wall. Monice pauses for a quick minute to let that marinate into her sense of thought. She then hears a car drive up into the driveway and notices that it is Gaylin, dressed in jean shorts with his hairy legs exposed .She rushes outside to speak to him.

"What's up, cousin? I love the scent of that appley air refresher." Monice said, as she walks up on him unexpectedly.

"Oh, girl, you almost scared me to death." He turns around and clutches his chest with his hand. "What are you doing here?" He continues grabbing bags from out the back seat.

"Visiting. I heard about your new engagement. I know you can't be serious," Monice shockingly said, all up in his face.

"Yes, I am," he said with attitude while walking towards the front door with the handful of shopping bags. "I love her."

"I don't see why you all have to get married so fast. It's only been a few days since you come from Connecticut. I think you should spend that money on something useful. I don't see what the big rush is."

"I love her and I want to be a father to my child." He snapped. "Now, go on home and leave me 'B'".

Monice said in a hostile tone as if she wanted to explode.

"Gail needs to find a job and stop sitting home every day watching those back biting soap operas!"

"So what? As long as she doesn't let it interfere with our marriage."

"What's your problem, Monice?" Gail intervened, as she opens the front porch door for Gaylin who has a smug look on his face. "Are you jealous of Gaylin and me? I'm now number one in his life, so you better get use to that. There are going to be some changes around here. I'm tired of you and

Dion trying to rule things. From now on, I want you two to stay out of our business."

"The choice is yours, I'm outta here." Monice sighed deeply, while strolling to her car that is parked along the side of the road in front of the shabby house.

"Good! Why don't you let me help you?" *Bam!* Gail slams the front door.

On September 30, 1980, Gaylin and Gail are married at the cathedral in Miami, Florida. Gail decided to have a bigger and romantic ceremony surrounded by family and friends. Monice, Dion and Gail's mother were not present, but they wished the best for something that might be the worst.

Four:
Misery Loves Company

Gaylin and Gail were united as one and planned to have the happiest time with the birth of their new baby in a few weeks. They moved into a luxury two-story home in a wealthy community, surrounded by doctors and lawyers. Gail hasn't spoken to Dion lately, simply because of how she feels about Gaylin.

"Honey, are you returning to your old job on Monday?" Gaylin said, with a strange look on his face, calmly reaching for the cigarette pack that is on the coffee table.

"No, I don't think so. With this baby due in a few weeks, I think I should stay close around the house and don't smoke in here, it's bad for the unborn baby," she said, while wobbling to the sofa chair with the latest fashion magazine in her hand.

"You need to get your lazy behind up and find a job!" He walks over to her and snatches the magazine out of her hand, with the lit cigarette dangling from the corner of his lips. "I can't support you forever!"

Gail looked with her mouth partially opened as though she had seen a ghost.

"You know the doctor advised me to stay off my feet."

"I don't care what the doctor said! The doctor doesn't pay the bills around here!" He shouted. "Get off your butt and look for a job!"

"All other men take care of their pregnant wives," she said. "You should take a few lessons from your buddy, Craig Mathis. He is a good man who takes care of his family."

Gail gloomily attempts to walk into the bedroom, but Gaylin raised his hand and eyed his wife, "What did you just say? Woman! Don't you ever compare me to another man!

You got that?! You're living off my money and my time! I was the one that took your sorry butt out of the hood and moved you into this rich neighborhood! Don't you ever forget the hand that feeds you!"
Gail dismisses his statement by a wave of the hand.
"Whatever. I'm going to bed." She strolls out headed straight to the bedroom.

Seeing red and lips curled as if he had a bad taste in his mouth, he runs and jerks Gail by her collar and pushes her against the wall.

"Don't you ever talk back to me, woman! I'll knock your head clean off your body!"

Monice later arrives at the residence when everything had simmered down between the battling couple. She had much gossip to tell him about his new bride. She notices that he is furiously sitting alone in the living room staring at a blank television screen.

"Hey, cousin, what's been going on?" She said, while stepping into the house from the front door that is unlocked.

"Monice, you need to knock before coming into someone's house."

"Oh… What's your problem?"

"Monice, I really don't feel like talking."

"I didn't drive all the way over here for you to turn me around. Now, talk to me. What's going on?"

Gaylin's fingers rubbed upward, past his forehead.

"It's Gail. We haven't been married a week and we're already fussing. She had the nerves to compare me to that old bumpy face, snaggle-tooth Craig Mathis who can't seem to talk right without stuttering."

"You got to be kidding," Monice said, as she attentively listens. "Craig Mathis?"

"Yeah, that heifer had the nerves. I wanted to slap the taste out of her mouth. She must don't know who she's messing with."

"Cousin, that's why I'm here,. The news is out all over the salon that Gail is not planning on finding a job. She is bragging to the girls in the shop that her husband is a famous movie star who makes a load of cash. I think family business should stay between families. Don't you think?" Gaylin walks into the kitchen and grabs a can of beer out of the refrigerator.

"I'm really tired of talking about Gail. Here's a cold beer for old time sake." Gaylin tosses the can of beer to Monice who is still sitting in the living room.

Monice had gathered her things and left the house before Gail arrived home drenched in sweat from walking two miles around the track of a local high school. The doctor advised her that walking was good for her pregnancy and that she should do it every day before going into labor. When she walks into the chilly dark house, she turns on a light and looks around and does not see Gaylin.

"Gaylin! I'm home!"

She slowly sits down on the sofa and takes off her sweaty athletic shoes.

"Gaylin!" She shouted, staring towards the stairs.

No response was heard. She then gets up and heads upstairs to the bedroom and looks around, feeling more uneasy when she notices that his car is still parked in the garage.

Her heart starts to pound and bad thoughts begin to enter her mind. Gail then walks into every room in the house and found it to be empty. For several minutes, she stood there in total shock, wondering where her husband could be without his car. She races into the kitchen and looked on the refrigerator door for a note and found nothing. Gail impatiently sits near the telephone and hopes that Gaylin would call.

While she is sitting, she hears the engine of a Mustang speeds out of the driveway. She rushes to the door and Gaylin then walks into the house, smelling like liquor and cheap perfume.

"Isn't that's Monice's car?" Gail questioned. "Where on earth have you been? I've been worried sick."

"Out," he nonchalantly said, in a bitter tone.

"Out where? You smell like a liquor bottle and cheap perfume. Where have you been?"

Gaylin walked past her without a care to what she was saying. He walks upstairs to the bathroom, closes the door and turns on the shower. The loud sound of bare feet stomps up the stairs. Gail bangs on the door with her fist.

"Didn't you hear me?" *Bang! Bang!* She continues to bang on the bathroom door with a balled fist. "Where have you been?"

Gail heard the water in the shower stop and then the door flung open.

"Get off my back, will you?" He said, water dripping off his chest onto the floor.

"I asked you a question and I want an answer! Where have you been, smelling like an old wino and stank perfume?"

"You really want to know! Yeah… I and my cousin were out having a few drinks at a club and I met my biggest fan who rubbed her nice big breast against my shirt while I was signing autographs!"

Gail had an incredulous look on her face.

"That's some real honesty for your butt! Now leave me the heck alone!" He said, as he slams the bathroom door shut and gets back into the shower.

The following day, Gail decides to enroll in college and obtain an early childhood degree. She also went back to her old high school seasonal job at the factory. She feels as though the family could use the extra money since the baby is due soon. But as she walks into the factory's office to fill out an application, she notices a woman sitting at the front desk, gathering papers that are unorganized. Gail smiles and walks slowly as she looks around and sees familiar faces.

"Hello, may I help you?"

"Yes, my name is Gail Harris. I worked here on last year, but I had to quit because of personal reasons. I would like to reapply for my former position."

"Well, you have to go through the entire hiring process. There's no such thing as a former position. Here is your application," the lady rudely said. Gail sat at the table and proceeded to apply for the job.

The woman mumbled underneath her breath as she watched Gail. "That's that famous movie star's girl. I see he didn't choose her for her looks."

Within a few minutes, Gail submitted her job application. The lady then glimpses over the application while she smacks on chewing gum. "Is 'the' Gaylin Harris your man?" She said in excitement, leaning over to hear the response.

"Yes, he is," Gail said as she stood up straight as possible.

"Hah, hah. I dated him in high school. He's Mr. Big Time, now, all up in Hollywood with the big dogs. I should holler and slip him my number. It's enough of him to go around. You know what I mean," the lady said very disrespectfully, smiling from ear to ear.

"Too late, he's all mine," Gail said sarcastically, flashing her Karat gold wedding ring in the lady's face.

"A wedding ring has never stopped a man," the woman said with a bold voice, looking at Gail with a slight grin.

Gail's pleasant attitude suddenly turned sour. She left the office very angry and dismal as she sits inside her car in ninety-five degree temperature with the windows up, meditating on the word of God: *"Be ye angry, and sin not: let not the sun go down upon your wrath. Neither give place to the devil."* – Ephesians 4:26

"Wherefore, my beloved brethren, let every man be swift to hear, slow to speak, slow to wrath." – James 1:19

She rested her palms on her forehead before being rudely disturbed by the lady in the office tapping on her window.

"Mrs. Harris. Are you available to start to work on next week?"

Gail immediately feels a release of happiness flow through her spirit.

"Yes. I can start right now if you need me," Gail stated.

The woman smiles and adjusts her miniskirt before speaking as she smacks on the chewing gum.

"That won't be necessary. Be here sharp on Monday morning at seven-thirty. Don't forget to purchase a hairnet and rubber boots."

Gail feels revived with excitement about getting her old job back as she drives down the highway singing gospel songs. Early Monday morning, Gaylin drives her to work in his exotic black 1980 Chevrolet Corvette. When he drives up to the curvy walkway for Gail to get out, he sees a tall, slender lady standing in the doorway, smoking a cigarette.

He then rushed Gail out of the car as if he didn't want the lady to see him.

"I'm late for my business meeting! Don't wait up for me tonight! I will grab dinner at Burger Land!" He said, while slightly shoving her out the car. She attempted to kiss him on the cheek but he moved away.

"Get out, now! I'm running late!"

"Not even a kiss?" She said, moving back closer to him as he waves her off in anger.

Gail then hurriedly gets out of the car without looking back. She walks into the factory where people were standing in a long line signing an attendance sheet. The tall slender woman walks to the car while straightening her short miniskirt.

"Hey stranger, I haven't seen you in a while."

"Yeah, it's been quite some time. You still look sexy."

"You're married, now?" The woman said, as she looks towards the factory's door. "Mr. Playboy who had all the women has tied the knot."

"It's not like that. She's just with me on borrowed time and then I'm tossing her butt back to the streets," he said. "I can do better."

"I don't have to report to work until ten o'clock. How about we ride off and make up for old time sake?" The lady said, laughing. "I really missed you over the years."

Gaylin looks down at his watch before speaking. A brown skin, husky built lady was standing from afar on the outside, observing everything she could.

"Let's go where we can have some privacy. I can spare a few minutes. I'm all about having fun," he said, as the lady gets into the car and he drives away in high speed.

The husky built lady who was standing outside on a smoke break saw the lady get into Gaylin's car. The employee waited until the car left the premises before she revealed the news.

The woman told Gail as she worked diligently beside her.

"You know that girl Veronica is fooling around with your man. I saw her get into his car."

Gail looked with a puzzled look and replied, "You have it all wrong. My husband left right after he dropped me off. You must saw someone else that had the same kind of car."

"If I were you, I'll go and wait outside for her. Let your own eyes be your witness," the lady laughed and said, as she packed the undergarment in a box.

Gail thought to herself and continued to work diligently. The lady speaks again after she didn't receive a positive response from Gail.

"If I were you, I'll put a stop to that Veronica. She sleeps around with everyone's man. About a month ago, a woman on the job caught her in the back warehouse with her husband. She almost beat the living crap out of that girl. Now you go outside and let your own eyes be your witness," the lady said again with much content.

The more Gail listened to the co-worker, the more convinced she was to take a break and go outside. She later went outside and waited for Gaylin to bring the girl back. She waited for thirty minutes and the lady shouted from the doorway.

"She doesn't have to be back until ten o'clock! Tell the supervisor that you have a family emergency and I will cover for you!"

"Are you playing some kind of joke? I don't have time for foolishness! I'm here to do a job and don't have time to stir up mess!" Gail speaks in anger with spit flying from her mouth.

"Let your own eyes be your witness. That young heifer needs her butt kicked. She's always walking around here with her nose up in the air like she's Miss America."

"I'm not the one to keep up mess. How do you know it was my husband? Are you sure?"

"Yes, I'm sure. I bet she's doing him right now. You better put your boxing gloves on, because when she arrives back, smelling like your man's cologne, you will be ready to pull all that fake horse hair out of her head."

Gail walked back into the building and continued to work. She worked until ten o'clock and proceeded to go back outside. But as she walked towards the door, the girl walked inside and looked at Gail with a smirk on her face. She sarcastically brushed against Gail's shoulders.

"Look girl, don't push my buttons!" Gail yelled in anger with both hands on her hips.

"Oh, I think your husband has already pushed mine, and it felt good, too."

Gail slapped the bony-framed girl in the face with an opened hand and then walked proudly back to her working area where middle-aged ladies were standing around laughing and cheering her on, especially the heavy weight gossiper that related the news. Within several minutes, the factory's security guard and supervisor approached her.

"Gail Harris?" The supervisor said, looking at her. "Come with me, please."

"What did I do?" Gail said her voice light and nervous.

"I have witnesses that stated you struck an employee in the face for no reason at all. We don't tolerate that kind of behavior here," the gray-haired man said before spitting tobacco juice in a plastic cup he is holding.

"That girl said some cruel things to me. I'm sorry that I lost my temper. Please give me another chance," Gail pleaded in tears. "I need my job." The nosy factory workers attentively stare at Gail and the supervisor.

"No, you must leave the premises," the man said. "If you don't, we will have to call the local police and have you arrested. Is that clear?"

Gail left the factory and walked to a nearby store. She phoned her mother and asked her to come and pick her up before noon. Three weeks later, Gail was rushed to the hospital to give birth to her child. Gaylin was out of town working on another movie and at the time, he was not aware of the birth. Dion phoned the movie producer at the hotel and tried to leave a message for Gaylin, but he was not interested in coming home to be with his wife and new baby.

Dion went back into the emergency room and stayed near Gail while she gave birth to her baby. Within twelve hours, Gail had given birth to a beautiful, eight-pound baby girl. The next day, Gail's mother, relatives and close friends came to visit. But Gaylin's relatives did not come, nor did they call. Gail sat in the chair and held her daughter as she longed for her husband, who was out and about getting drunk and enjoying himself with evil people who cared less about moral values and Christian living.

Five:
Double Trouble

It's been almost twenty years since the birth of Gail's daughter, Lyndia, who is now a sophomore in college. The family still resides in Miami and Gaylin's career as an actor failed one decade ago due to his flirtatious behavior that caused him a numerous sexual assault charges. Although his wife never knew the true reason for his dismissal, he still kept a professional job to support his family. Gail is a fifth-grade middle school teacher at Dunwood Middle School.

Dion, all dressed up in a black, strapless dress with the matching high-heel pumps, struts into Gail's energetic fifth-grade classroom as if she was another teacher in the hallway. It's the first month of another new school year.

Knock, knock.

Gail surprisingly looks back towards the door.

"Dion, what are you doing here? Is everything okay?"

"Look, girl." Dion walks in and flashes a diamond ring in Gail's face.

"Wow! He proposed. That son of a gun finally proposed," Gail happily said, as she covers her mouth in embarrassment when she realizes that her students were being very attentive.

"Class, continue to read chapter seven. I'll be back in a moment." Gail and Dion walk quietly out into the hallway to finish talking.

"I'm getting married," never thought I would ever say that word."

"Yeah. You're doing the right thing. Shacking up with a man is not the way God instructs," Gail said. "Marriage is a good thing if you're with the right one."

"Yes, it is. But in your case, Gail, I think you struck out."

"Don't come out here with that mess, Dion. I thought we left that in the past." Gail utters with a frown. "I have a class to teach. Congratulations on your new engagement. "

Twelve o'clock noon arrives and Gail's fifth- grade class has rejuvenated from spending one hour in gym class, running around releasing all the pinned up energy. It is time for lunch and Gail escorts all fifteen students to the restroom to wash up.

"Mrs. Harris, what's for lunch today?" a young, freckled face, white boy said who is standing in line waiting for the other kids to come out.

"I don't know, Tommy," she said as she stands firmly with her hands on her hips.

"I hope it's not fish. We had fish on Monday," he said in disgust.

"Tommy, it's not nice to be ungrateful. So what if you're eating fish again. There are so many children who are hungry and don't have food to eat. Doesn't your mother teach you anything?"

"No, she's too busy with that man who brings you to school." The boy covers his mouth. "Oops, I wasn't supposed to say anything."

"Don't worry about it. It's not your fault." She blinked eyes full of tears.

Gail turned away suddenly, her eyes still filled with tears. While she waited for all her students to come out of the restroom, she reached in her bag for an aspirin. She had developed a slight headache from hearing from a fifth-grader that her husband is having an affair.

They soon arrived into the cafeteria with the aroma of hot beef stew and seasoned vegetables illuminating through the air. Gail walks her class through the lunch line and she immediately prepares herself a big bowl of hot stew. With angry vicious thoughts of her husband in mind, she carelessly strolls to the teacher's table and accidentally drops the bowl of steaming hot soup on a teacher who is sitting at the end of the row.

"Ouch!" The lady shockingly jumps up, breathing deeply as she tries to get the hot food off her clothes.

"Oh, my God! I'm so sorry. Let me help." Gail apologetically states, grabbing napkins and wiping the tomato sauce, green beans and corn from off the lady's wet, beautiful, cotton shirt.

"It's okay. I'll do it," The lady said in frustration.

"No, I insist. I was very clumsy and wasn't paying attention to where I was going. Here, take these napkins," Gail said with concern, handing the woman a handful of white paper napkins. "Do you have any burns?"

"Really, it's okay. It's not the first time someone spilled hot soup on me. I guess I should try out for the 'hot soup lap awards'," the lady jokingly said with a smile. "By the way, I'm Saddie Florence." She extends her wet hand in greeting.

"I'm Gail Harris. It's a pleasure to meet you." The two women then sit down at the table where an entrée of beef stew is sitting in front of them.

"Are you new? I've never seen you here before?" Gail asked Saddie, as she prepares herself another bowl of soup.

"Girl, where have you been? No, I'm not new. I've been here almost three years. Saddie quickly stated, still wiping the food from her clothes.

"Three years? I must have been staying inside my classroom too long! I need to stop grading these papers every day and get out more! I'm so sorry for mistaking you for a new teacher," Gail said, sipping a glass of lemon water.

"Please get out and tour your school more often before you smother yourself in class work," Saddie giggled. "The school could be on fire and you won't know it."

"Are you going to introduce me, Saddie?" Another teacher who is also sitting at the table intervenes.

"Oh, yeah, this is my dear friend Nadine Lacrow," Saddie said with a wide smile.

"How are you?" Nadine extends her hand to Gail in greeting.

Saddie and Nadine are both from Georgia who recently graduated from a University in Miami. Saddie is very beautiful and outgoing with a nice slim figure. Her eyes are gray and very hypnotic to men. Her buttery, smooth, vanilla skin is very radiant, and pleasing to touch. She loves to wear exotic hairstyles and sexy outfits that lure attention. Nadine, on the other hand, is more like Gail, very ordinary, stodgy, and has an inner beauty that's extremely pleasing to God.

While Gail was sitting conversing with the two women, she heard her name being called over the intercom system. Gail excused herself and walked to the principal's office. When she walked in, she noticed Gaylin sitting at the table reading a magazine. The thought of what her student said about his mother and Gaylin entered her mind.

"Is everything okay?" Gail said with a forced smile, clenched teeth.

"I need to borrow the car. I let Roscoe use mine to take Dion out on a romantic outing."

"No, you can't borrow my car. I need my vehicle to run errands when I get off today," she said rudely, trying to walk out of the office.

"Where do you think you're going?" He tried to block her path with his one hundred ninety-pound body frame. "I'm the one that paid for the car. I just let you borrowed it."

"You think you can throw up in my face every time you spend a lousy dime on me!" She reaches inside her pocket and tosses the keys at him. "Here, take the car! I don't need your chump change anymore!" Gail loudly shouted, as workers in the office slightly observe without staring.

"Let's not make a scene, baby. All I want is the car so I can go and take care of some business. I'll be back to get you. As a matter of fact, I'll be back before school's out," he said as he kisses her on the cheek.

While Gail attempts to leave the office, Saddie and Nadine walk inside. Saddie yelled as she watched Gaylin stroll to the car.

"Who's that fine hunk? Brother man got it going on!"

"That's my husband you're talking about. That's my fine and sexy man." Gail answered with pride.

"That's good, girlfriend. Let a woman know whose man he is," Saddie jokingly said as she looks at Nadine.

"He looks familiar. Where did you meet him?" Saddie questioned, still watching Gaylin from the office window.

"You've probably have seen him on television commercials some time ago. He worked as an actor with top named celebrities back in the late seventies and early eighties."

"Seventies, honey, I was still running around in pee-pee diapers still scared of the boogieman back then," she said. "You got yourself one good looking man."

"Don't let them looks fool you. He isn't all that great. He makes mistakes just like all the rest," Gail said. "But, I'm a forgiving person." She thinks of what her student said about him.

"I know that's right. Black men these days can't be trusted. They're no good! All they do is tell lies, screw you, and then get you pregnant and claim that they're not the father!" Saddie said. "That's why I'm getting an Asian man; all they do is cook rice."

"All men aren't dogs. I trust my husband," Gail said, feeling dishearten.

"Yeah, right, I'll trust him as far as I see him," Saddie told her. "Now let's go get our snot nose students before we be without jobs." The women then leave the office and walk back to their classroom.

The workday is over and Gail waits patiently outside the school for Gaylin. She waited for several hours until she noticed that her sporty ride was parked on the other side of the building.

"Oh, I forgot that he said that the car would be here."

Saddie drives near Gail's parked car with Nadine on the passenger side. Gail attempts to get into her car.

"Ooh! Nice set of wheels," Saddie said, admiring Gail's shiny Red Corvette. "Come ride with me to take Nadine home."

"I can't right now. I have to cook dinner and get things ready for tomorrow," Gail replied back while opening her car door.

"You're already late. A few extra minutes won't hurt anything," Saddie said, trying to convince Gail to take a ride.

"How did you know that I was still here? School has been out for almost two hours!" Gail asked.

"We saw you standing on the steps when I passed by on my way to the gas station. Why are you still here?" Saddie asked with concern.

"I've been waiting for my husband to bring me the vehicle. I didn't know that it was already here parked around the building. I have a lot of things to do at home. Thanks for the offer," Gail said as she gets into her automobile.

"I told you not to let him borrow your car. You may need to check that passenger seat for open condom wrappers and Vaseline."

"That wasn't nice to say, Saddie. I think you should apologize to Gail," Nadine spoke.

"I'm just joking around. Once Gail gets to know me, she'll find out that I'm very outgoing."

"Well, okay. I'll go just this one time. Now, have me back to this car before dark."

Gail got into the car and Saddie drove off very fast.

"So, where are we going?" Gail asked, looking down at her watch.

"Your mind must be bad. I told you earlier that I was taking Nadine home. But first, I got to make a quick stop.

"Make it quick because I got to have dinner ready before my husband gets home," Gail sighed. "He hates when dinner is late."

"That's why I'm glad that I don't have excess baggage of a husband lingering on behind me. Men are like babies, always wanting to be pampered. I don't have time to please only one man. Marriage is not for me. I love my freedom," Saddie happily said, as she runs her fingers through her nice, long brown hair.

Saddie giggles and then drives into the parking lot of the county jail where prisoners were standing out on the outside performing work duty.

"I thought we were taking Nadine home? Why are we at the county jail?"

"I'm going to visit my boyfriend, Alfredo," she said, while parking the car in the visitor's parking space. "Today is the only day I can visit before he goes to prison for beating the crap out of his wife with a baseball bat."

"His wife?" Gail questioned. "So, you're fooling around with a married man?"

"Don't take it personal. I enjoy what I do because there is no commitment. I sleep with them, spend their money, and then send them back home to their boring wives. No pain, no shame."

"You're committing adultery! You're going straight to hell!" Gail shouted, spit flying out of her mouth.

"No, darling, it's only adultery when you're married and break the vows. I haven't crossed that line, yet," Saddie said.

"Whatever. Sin is sin in God's eyesight. You should be ashamed of yourself," Gail said as she attempts to open the car door.

"Why are you getting so bent out of shape about it? It's almost the new millennium. Everyone's doing it. You should step out and get you a piece of fresh meat sometime." Saddie looked at Gail from head to toe. "Don't tell me you haven't been tempted."

"I dare you! Let me out of this car!" Gail shouted, while forcefully trying to open the locked door.

"Calm down. There's no need to get hysterical. It's not like I'm looking at your man. I don't fool around with my friend's men."

"You're no friend of mine! You're just a gold digging slut who can't find her own man!" Gail said, looking serious. "Open this door!"

Gail gets out of the car and proceeds to walk back to the school. Nadine races behind her and yells for her to stop walking.

"Gail, don't leave! Saddie is really a good person!" Nadine yelled. "I've been trying to get her on the right track for a long time! She's only doing this because she is searching for love in all the wrong places!"

"I don't care! That doesn't give her a reason to fool around with married men!" Gail shouted back, very offensively.

"True! But she's doing it for revenge! Trust me. She doesn't enjoy sleeping around with different men!" Nadine said, almost out of breath from shouting from afar.

"I can sympathize with these women because I'm a married woman, too! She's sleeping with men after they have slept with their wives! That's so gross!" Gail angrily shouted back.

"Stop, don't walk so fast! Just hear what I'm trying to say!" Nadine breathlessly said, while aggressively inhaling and exhaling air from her lungs.

Gail then stops walking and Nadine runs to talk to her.

"Let's go back to the car and pray for Saddie. We as Christians can't turn our backs on her. We must continue to spread God's word and hope that she will change for the best," stated Nadine.

"I don't know. I got to think about it," Gail bitterly said, arms fold across her chest.

"Think about it? What if God had to think about it every time we did something wrong. We're supposed to live our life as God would want us to. We're not perfect," Nadine said, as she quickly covered her face in disappointment.

"You're right. I must forgive Saddie and try to help her. I didn't mean to come off so harshly," Gail said, giving Nadine a slight caring hug.

They both walked back to the car and waited for Saddie to come out of the crowded building with prisoners walking around while the guards are near their side. Saddie later got back into the car and was very angry with frown lines all in her face.

She said angrily with a balled fist, "That woman will not get away with this. Alfredo is mine and I'm not going to lose him over no bull mess!"

Nadine looked at Gail and then at Saddie before stating.

"Alfredo isn't your man to lose. Wait on God, he'll send you someone."

"Are you crazy, Nadine? God did send me a good man and what did he do? That no good faggot preferred to be cuddled up at night with another dude! Yeah, I caught my ex-husband bumping and grinding with a man, right on our living room floor. He's lucky that I only had one bullet in that gun."

"Oh, I didn't know you were once married. Don't blame yourself for his loss. God will send you another husband, but you have to stop what you're doing. Don't continue to allow these men to abuse your lovely temple that God created. You're special. You don't have to settle for less. There are a few good men who are searching for good women. Come to church with me on Sunday and we will pray for strength," Gail said, as she gives Saddie a motherly hug.

"That man shattered my life. It took almost a year to get over his sorry butt."

"You'll be okay," Gail replied. "You'll get over it. The Bible speaks clearly on adultery. Those wedding vows should be taken seriously. Anyone who violates those vows has violated their promise to God."

"I'll come to church with you, but it will take some time for me to change. I can't do it overnight. I have to wait until I'm fully ready to commit myself."

"Okay, but don't wait too late. We don't know how much time we have on earth. Don't put off for tomorrow what can be done today. If God allows you a second chance to make it right then do it. The cemetery is full of unsaved people wishing for another chance to do things differently. Take my advice and listen," Gail said with concern.

The women leave the county jail and drive back to the school where Gail's car is parked. Gail gets into her car and drives away. She turns on her radio and begins listening to gospel music, bouncing her head to the rhythm, as she cruises down the busy street. She notices her sporty car beginning to pick up speed. So she slowly begins pushing down on the brakes, but the car went even faster, swerving across the street as if it was demon possessed. Gail starts panicking and then she pulls up the emergency brake, but that didn't stop the car either.

Gail starts crying and yelling, "Someone help me! Someone please help me!"

She presses the car horn and sees pedestrians running in the opposite direction. Suddenly, she comes upon heavy traffic at a busy intersection and strikes a parked bus from behind on the curve. The small vehicle is pinned underneath the bus.

People get out of their automobiles and then call 911. A man runs to the scene very attentive and nervous. "Oh no, Let me call for help!"

Within ten minutes, the ambulance, police officers and the firemen were at the horrible scene, directing traffic to another direction. While the fire fighters were trying to cut the roof off the severely smashed sports car, the paramedics waited patiently to rush Gail to the emergency room. A police officer checks the car's tags and registration for possible identification and then calls Gail's home to inform her husband about the accident.

Ring, ring. Gaylin looks over at the telephone on the nightstand that is constantly ringing.

"Hello, who is this?"

"This is Officer Blake. Your wife has been in a terrible car accident here downtown on Ridge and Holt Road. She will be transported to the local hospital. We need you here as soon as possible."

"Oh… okay." *Click.* Gaylin hangs up the telephone.

He then lies back in the bed at his house, takes a sip of red wine that is on the nightstand, and turns on some soft music.

"Now baby, let's finish what we started before we were rudely interrupted." Gaylin was in his wife's bed at home, snuggled up with another woman.

Six:
Cheating in My Bedroom

It was half-past eight at night before Gail was transported to the hospital with internal bleeding, a broken spine, fractured ribs and a dislocated shoulder. The lady kisses, caresses, and speaks softly in Gaylin's ear while he strokes her body with his strong big hands.

"Who was that on the telephone?"

"No one important," He said nonchalantly, running his fingers through the lady's beautiful hair.

"Not important? That man on the other end sure thought so. Come on tell me? I heard him say something about a Gail. Now what's going on?" She demanded with attitude.

"Okay…Gail is my wife who was in a terrible car accident."

"What? Oh my God! We must get there! Give me the phone and let me call to see how she's doing!" The lady shouted, as she sprung up off the full-size bed and fumbled around the bedroom for her clothes.

"Are you crazy? She doesn't know you! You're not going anywhere. All hell would break loose if someone suspects something about us," He snapped. "Go on home and I'll call you later."

Gail was listed in critical condition after she went under six-hours of surgery.

Dion ran hysterically into the emergency room wearing a headscarf, an old dress and bedroom shoes after she said she heard about the accident from a neighbor who was standing along the sidewalk, biting her nails at the scene of the accident. Dion was crying and hoped the best. Gaylin later arrived to the hospital dressed up wearing a pimped out brown suit.

"Hello, I heard that my wife was in a car accident. Can someone show me her room?" He said to a nurse at the front desk trying to show concern.

"What is your wife's name, sir? We have a lot of hospitalized women here," The nurse stated, looking down at a list of names.

"Her name is Gail Harris. She was in an accident that happened on the main intersection between Ridge and Holt Road," he bitterly said, glancing around the emergency room.

"She's in surgery. The doctor will be over to talk to you shortly. Just have a seat in the waiting area," the nurse stated, signaling him in that direction.

Hours later, the doctor finally comes up front to speak to him about his wife. Gaylin is sitting in a chair engaging in conversation with a man about his job.

"Mr. Gaylin Harris?" The doctor said, looking at the two men trying to determine which one was he.

"You're looking at him," Gaylin proudly said, waving his hand.

"I am glad you made it. Your wife is in critical condition. You can see her as soon as we find her a room in the critical ward," Dr. Walter said gently, adjusting his clipboard.

Dion overheard the conversation and walked near Gaylin. She yelled in anger as she slapped him in the face with an opened hand.

"You're going to pay for this!" She angrily said. "This is your fault!"

Gaylin forcefully shoved Dion against the hard wall and Roscoe intervened as he grabbed Gaylin.

"Hey man, don't lose your cool on my wife! Let me handle this!"

"You better get your wife before I put this size-fifteen shoe up her butt!"

Roscoe pulled Dion aside and said, "What's wrong with you? You had no right slapping that man in his face."

"He's behind all of this! I just know it! He drove her to do this!" Dion said, tears flowing down her smooth cheek.

"What do you mean? He drove her to do what?" Roscoe asked, staring at his wife right in the face.

"I think Gail tried to kill herself. There is no way she would have accidentally run her car into a parked bus on the side of the road. She must was upset about something and that something is her low-down, dirty husband."

"Tell you what," Roscoe said, pulling his wife by the arm and escorting her to an empty chair. "If you promise me that you'll lay off Gaylin, I'll treat you to a delicious steak dinner tomorrow night at your favorite restaurant. Deal?"

"You don't know the whole story. That man has been trouble since day one. He is a snake in the grass. He is sneaky and is a low-down, dirty dog," Dion said in tears while wiping her runny nose with the back of her hand.

"Don't bad mouth the man. What goes on in his house is none of our business. Let's go home, we can't do too much for Gail out here in this waiting room," Roscoe said, as he helps Dion out of the chair and they proceed to walk out of the hospital.

"Not so fast! What's the big hurry?" Monice said, strutting into the hospital with frown lines all in her face.

"We would love to stay, but Dion is all emotional and I don't think she needs to be here, stirring up her nerves. Just call us if Gail's condition changes," Roscoe said, sounding sorrowful.

Monice then walked over to Gaylin and plopped down in a chair next to him.

"Are you okay? What did they say about Gail?" she questioned with concern.

Gaylin stood up and replied with his left foot propped against the wall, "The doctor said that she's not doing well."

"What happened? I just got a call that she was in an accident."

"Yeah. Somehow or another, she just wrecked my brand-new Corvette! I just bought it a few months ago! She better have a darn good excuse for wrecking my car!" He harshly stated while his eyes beamed in anger.

"Don't worry about the car, you'll get another one. It's Gail who you should be concerned about," Monice sympathetically speaks.

"Gail, my behind! I don't give a rat's butt about how she's doing! I believe she wrecked my car on purpose because the other night she found a perfume bottle on the floor!" He said, looking serious.

"Grab a whole of yourself before you lose your cool!" Monice said emotionally, shaking him by his shoulders. "Now, you know Gail wouldn't do anything like that. She loves you and you should try to show a little respect during a time like this. She needs you."

Several hours have passed and the doctor allowed Gaylin into his wife's room. The doctor told him before he entered her room, that Gail's spine was severely damaged, but he would refer her to an orthopedist so that she could receive proper care and be able to walk again. A sudden sense of rage had come forth. Gaylin's eyebrows rise in anger as he clenches his teeth before speaking.

"No, I'm not getting her a specialist. I don't have the money to keep paying higher health insurance. She wouldn't be in this mess if she had had her black behind home. I didn't get my dinner because of this." Gaylin argued.

"Sir, things like this sometimes happen. Money should not be an issue when it comes to life or death situations. You can apply for low income. Some health agencies have a sliding scale for people who desperately need the assistance, but can't afford the services. I'll give you the forms to fill out, so that your services can start immediately," Dr. Walter stated in a caring tone, looking at Gaylin seriously.

"She'll be okay. I'm not applying for low income. The minute those people see my check stub they'll have me responsible for Gail's bill. I'm not going to do it. She can sign herself up for disability and learn how to use the wheelchair like other sick invalids," Gaylin argued, glancing around the hallway at patients in wheelchairs.

"What? You can't be serious," Dr. Walter said while scratching his bald scalp in disbelief. "You'll rather see your wife in a wheelchair before you sign a few documents for her to see an Orthopedist? That is cruel. I won't allow it. I simply will not allow it!"

"There's no law that states I have to get in debt for a specialist! She's my wife and I said that she's not seeing an orthopedist! Now you better do your job or get ready to lose it because if you keep pressuring me I will see you in court!" Gaylin shouted with an attitude.

Gaylin then walked into his wife's room and kissed her on the cheek. He spoke softly as he pulled back her thick, blue blanket from underneath her arms. "Hey baby. I love you so much. How are you feeling?"

Gail's big brown eyes opened widely and she replied softly in a weak tone, "Hi, sweetheart."

Gaylin begins crying and pacing around the room as if he felt guilty for not being beside his wife during this terrible crisis.

"Baby, I wanted to be here. I tried to get here, but my boss kept giving me bogus excuses for not leaving. I'm so sorry for being late." He hugged his wife as tears felled down her face.

"It's okay. Thank God you're here now," she said in a weak tone, very softly.

One month later, on a beautiful, sunny Tuesday morning around nine o'clock, the doctor comes into Gail's hospital room with more devastating news to tell her about her health. Her mother was feeding her buttered grits and fried ham when the doctor arrived.

"Well, hello, Mrs. Harris. I see you're up, bright and early. How has everything been going?"

"Sort of stiff and is tired of this bed, but other than that, I'm blessed," she said, flashing a wide smile.

"Mrs. Harris, there's something that I must tell you. I hate to inform you, but your spine is severely damaged and you will have to see an orthopedist in order to walk again. I told your husband about this a few weeks ago but he refuses to seek help," Dr. Walter stated, seriously. "Also, you are pregnant."

"Pregnant? Specialist? Broken spine? Wait one minute, doc. You're throwing too much at her at one time. Let's start over," Gail's mother said, very confused.

"No, Mama, I understand quite well. I'm pregnant! That's a blessing that came at the right time!" Gail said, as she rubs her stomach that is bandaged up.

"Doc, didn't you say that her spine was broken? So my baby is not going to walk again." Gail's mother sadly uttered, as she walks near Doctor Walter.

"That's correct. She has to see a specialist. Without serious medical help, she will not be able to walk. Her spine is damaged too bad."

Gail lies in bed covered up with a blanket, very heartbroken about her medical condition. Moments later, Gaylin parades into the room, all dressed up in a pair of crisply ironed jeans and a button-up designer shirt. He politely speaks to Gail's mother who is sitting in a rocking chair near her daughter's bed. He then places a warm kiss on his wife's cheeks.

"How could you? Why didn't you sign the forms for me to see a specialist?" Gail angrily questioned.

"Specialist? What you mean?" He said, trying to play dumb.

"A specialist for me to see about my spine, Dr. Walter came in and told me that he spoke with you about my condition. Why didn't you tell me?"

"Oh… We can't afford it now. I got to try to buy another Corvette. Baby, don't you know, I saw one today, a black one."

"Are you nuts? I'm here sick, lying up in a hospital bed with a damaged spine and all you can talk about is a car. You have some nerves."

"What? The insurance will pay for me another car. I got to have something sporty to get around in."

"What about my specialist?"

"What about it?"

"Gaylin, I can't walk! I need help, fast!"

"Gail, there's the wheelchair. I can't afford for my health insurance to go up. Don't you know a specialist would cost an arm and a leg?"

"So what? That's what the insurance is for; to use when you need it."

"Enough about that! You're not seeing a specialist and that's final! I'm not going to argue with you about my own money!" Gaylin snapped, looking at his wife who is staring at him with a frown.

"Fine! Oh, by the way, I'm pregnant! So, I guess now you can't get that new Corvette because we're going to need the money for the baby," she said sarcastically.

Gaylin paused, fumbles in his pocket before he burst out laughing.

"Ha, Ha. This is a joke, right? Look at you! You're too old to have another child! You're thirty-eight years old and will be in a wheelchair! I don't have time to nurse you and a baby! I think you're only doing this to get back at me! I will not stand for it! I want you to get rid of this baby!" Gaylin demanded, pointing a finger at her.

"No, Gaylin. I'm not trying to get back at you. I want my child," Gail cried. "I want to be a mother again. Lyndia is grown and has a life of her own in college. I'm not too old to carry this child."

"Look, Gaylin. My daughter is not getting rid of this baby, unless the good Lord himself snatches it out of her belly. Now, I've stayed quiet long enough and I'm not going to let you get rid of my grandchild!" Mrs. Bradford said, raising her voice.

"This is not your business," he said to her through his teeth.

"Oh yes, it is my business! This is my grandchild and I'm not going to let you talk my daughter into killing it!"

Gaylin stormed out of the room and slammed the door behind him, very hard. A nurse, who is passing by, offers her assistance.

"Are you okay, sir? What's wrong?" She questioned as she glanced at Gail's closed room door.

"Nothing!" He walks inattentively and tramples into a medicine cart that is sitting in the middle of the hallway. The nurse apologetically runs over to help.

"Are you okay, sir? I'm so sorry I left this here," she said, trying to help Gaylin off the floor.

For the next two months, Gail remained at the hospital with limited abilities to use her legs. She was placed in a wheelchair and received free daily therapy from physical therapy intern students who come around three days a week. Gaylin did not like that idea. In fact, he wanted to stop his wife's therapy sessions so that she could never learn how to walk again.

Gaylin steps outside the automatic business doors, dressed GQ-style wearing a denim designer shirt and tight blue jeans. The temperature in the high 90s welcomed him as he wipes his sweaty forehead with the back of his hand and walks abruptly to his vehicle. Once inside the car, he buckles his seat belt, pops a CD inside the disk track, and then places the dark sunglasses over his hazel-brown eyes and speeds off in his new sporty black Corvette.

Seven:
Millennium Madness

December 31, 1999 was not the typical day for television newscasters, world leaders, political camps and especially Gail Harris who has arrived home for the first time in months after she sustained injuries from her horrific car accident that nearly claimed her life. She and her mother arrive at the family church for watch night services to joyfully bring in a new millennium and a new beginning. Some people are out and about in shopping malls, grocery stores and the nightclubs preparing for the new upcoming century because they do not know what lies ahead.

A great deal of Americans feel as though the world will end without warning, but many believes that the Y2K bug will bring upon much confusion and chaos that will probably send people totally haywire. But not Christians, who have faith in God and knows for sure that no man on earth, angels in Heaven, or the Son of God himself, knows the time, day or hour the Lord shall come: and he is coming whether or not atheists or non-believers want to acknowledge it.

Sweet Temple Baptist Church is filled with Christians who are standing around, clapping and singing gospel hymns along with the angelical adult choir. It has been three months since Gail's accident, and she is now in church, giving God the praises for keeping her alive. She sits in the aisle in her wheelchair, next to her mother who is sitting on a pew. They both clap their hands in unison as the choir sings 'Someday.'

Pastor Willie Samuel stands in his heavenly chestnut pulpit behind his podium and welcomed the congregation to the house of the Lord this last day of the century. "Let's give honor to God who is the head of our lives. If it weren't for Him who woke us up this morning, we would not know where we would be today. Our God is an awesome God who gives us strength to defeat the enemy. I'm glad you all are here tonight on this last day of the century. There's no better place than being in the House of the Lord."

"Amen," a few people said in unison.

"Let us bow our heads in prayer before going into our regular worship service," Pastor Willie Samuel said bowing his head with his hands stretch out in the air.

"Heavenly Father, bless this congregation that stands before you. We are living in tough times and no one knows the day of your arrival. Many think it's tonight when the clock strikes twelve and a new century arrives, but no one knows. You will come like a thief in the night. No one knows when a thief will enter, but we must be ready. Heavenly Father, bless this upcoming century and bring new beginnings and changes to the world. Allow the crooked to be made straight, and the wicked to turn from their evil ways. Heavenly Father, bless the White House and bring about changes so that everyone can learn to live in harmony and peace."

"Amen. It's time for a black president," an elderly woman said, waving her hands to the Heavens.

"Heavenly Father, bless the non-believers and allow them to know you personally. Able those to know that their help comes from you and that you are God that will never fail. Heavenly Father, help the ones that does not know you personally and allow the Holy Spirit to guide their footsteps because the enemy is out on attack."

"Amen," the congregation said, clapping hands.

"Heavenly Father, bless marriages and let Satan know that he has no place between a husband and a wife, there's no room for a third wheel."

"Amen. Praise the Lord!" Gail shouted, clapping her hands in unison with the congregation.

"Heavenly Father, if the devil happens to deliver a problem or situation that we cannot handle, please take control because we know that you do not sleep nor do you slumber and there is no need for us to lose any sleep worrying about the things in this world."

"Hallelujah, praise the Lord!" An elderly lady shouted, standing up crying and waving her hands in the air.

"Heavenly Father, we thank you for providing food on our tables and clothes on our backs. Our pockets may be empty and our friends may be few. But Lord, as long as we got you as the head of our lives, we have everything. I just thank you for our prosperity and good health even as our soul prospers. We praise your Holy name."

While everyone had his or her head bowed down in prayer, Gaylin peers his angry face through the church door leading to the sanctuary. His eyes spot Gail and he then races in wearing a pimped out gray suit and shiny black shoes.

"Woman, let's split! I thought you were here!" Gaylin said loudly, tapping Gail on her shoulder, who is bowed down praying. She startles, looks up at him.

"Gaylin. What do you want?" She said quietly, looking around nervously. The preacher continues praying.

"Heavenly Father, bless this heartless, Satan dressed heathen that is trying to interrupt this watch night service. Amen" The pastor boldly stares at Gaylin.

The congregation shockingly gazes back at Gaylin who is angrily trying to push his wife's wheelchair out of the sanctuary. A husky built male usher at the front entrance intervenes as Gaylin forces Gail's wheelchair out the narrow doorway.

"Sir, we don't want any trouble in the House of the Lord. Can't you see that this lady does not want to go with you?"

"Shut up, partner and mind your own business! This is my wife, not yours!"

Gaylin continues to force Gail's wheelchair out the door. She is uncontrollably grabbing at his arms, trying to free his hands from the wheelchair.

"No, Gaylin. I'm not going?" Gail said, fumbling around in her chair. Her mother races behind him while he is pushing Gail's wheelchair out of the church.

"Hold up, sucker! Where do you think you're taking my child? Get your hands off her or I'm calling the police!" Mrs. Bradford demanded, pointing a finger.

"Call the police! This is my wife and what I say goes. I'm not going to have her mind all wrapped up in this church business. She needs to be home, cooking and cleaning for tonight. I have friends coming over and I'm not going to let them come to a dirty house!" He shouted back, still pushing the wheelchair.

As Gaylin and Gail made their way out the front door, two police cars drove up into the church parking lot. Apparently, someone in the church had reported a disturbance.

Gaylin stops immediately and whispers in Gail's ear, while gazing at the officers who are getting out of their cars, "Remember, I'm the hand that feeds you and I'm the hand that will knock you out!" Gail sits with tears flowing as her mother runs to the officers to tell what happened.

Later that night, right before New Year's Day, Gail wheels herself around in the lonely house, very sad in the way her husband had earlier behaved in the House of the Lord. He had gone out to a nightclub with a few of his office buddies to celebrate the upcoming year. Gail's mother had gone back to church since the police officers were not able to lawfully make Gail free herself from her devious husband. She was now hungry, cold and shivering with fear and was ready to go to bed. Gaylin had purposely left her sitting in the wheelchair, knowing that she needed assistance to bathe, eat and get in and out of bed.

Twelve o'clock came in briefly as people in the street begin cheering, sounding firecrackers and yelling towards the Heavens that a new millennium has arrived. Gail had slumped over and fallen asleep in her wheelchair. She is suddenly awakened by the loud noise that could be heard from afar. A tear rolls down her face as she thanks God for allowing her to see another new year. She soon dozes off into a deep sleep.

Early the next morning, around eight o'clock, the bright morning sunshine beams in on Gail's soft brown cheeks. She slowly awakes while drooling from the mouth with sleep still in her eyes and notices that she had slept the entire night in the off balance wheelchair. She shouted for her husband to come down stairs, but no answer.

Ring, ring. Gail looks at the ringing telephone that sits on a table near the television.

Ring, ring. She then wheels herself to answer it.

"Hello."

"Happy New Years!" Dion shouted, blowing a whistle in the earpiece.

"Ouch, girl! Stop blowing that darn whistle in my ear!"

"What's wrong with you? You should be thrilled that the sky isn't falling"

"No time for jokes this morning. I had to sleep all night in this narrow chair and I'm not up for laughter right now," Gail said, with frown lines in her face.

"Oh… I'm so sorry. You mean to tell me that no good man of yours left you up? Girl he sure was having fun last night, all up in some fat woman's face that was wearing a tight hoochie shirt with her flabby, stretch mark belly all hanging out."

"He was with a woman?" Gail asked, looking serious.

"Yeah, girl, a big fat one, Roscoe and I saw him at Club Dynamite last night. He was on the dance floor bumping and grinding with Mrs. Burger butt. That scum bag cared less about us seeing him," Dion said.

Gail held the telephone to her ear and there was total silence for a few seconds.

"Gail, are you still there?"

"Dion, I'm not feeling well. I'll talk to you later." *Click.* Gail disconnects the telephone call and sits silently in her wheelchair.

Gail wished for a quick moment that she could rewind twenty years of her life back and become that normal energetic teenager she once was, before she met Gaylin Harris. The thoughts brought bitterness and resentment in her spirit until she felt the presence of the Lord linger within. Therefore, she laid aside her ill feelings and began praising God for a new year.

The spirit from the Heavenly Father put a huge smile upon her face that made her forget all trouble that was burdening her heart. Although she was unable to walk and move abruptly upstairs in the house, she still operated the wheelchair and continued to do her wifely duties downstairs. Within fifteen minutes, the telephone began ringing again. Gail rolled herself into the living room and retrieved it.

"Happy New Years, Harris residence."

"Hello, may I please speak to Gaylin?" The unannounced speaker said. The voice sounded so familiar that Gail responded with a question.

"What? Who is this?"

The person speaks slowly as if they are trying to disguise their voice.

"Is Gaylin home? I need to speak with him."

Gail answered politely, "He's not here. May I take a message?"

Bang! The person then slammed the telephone down onto the receiver and the call was disconnected.

Gail thought that it was strange for some woman to call her home and demand to speak to her husband. She did not let the telephone call ruin her good morning, so she continued to do her housework. However, she went into the neatly decorated guest bedroom to dust the expensive furniture and there was an awful foul smell in the air. She looked on the floor beside the bed and came across a pair of dingy, stained bikini underwear that smelled like some woman forgot to take a fresh douche. She looked down at them before saying aloud.

"Where did this come from? I guess it must be Lyndia's," she said.

Lyndia is her daughter who is away in college, who comes home on some weekends to visit her parents. Gail then picked the undergarment up and placed it in the waste basket in the guest bathroom.

The telephone rang again and she became impatient and wheeled herself back into the living room. When she answered it, her daughter, Lyndia was on the other end.

"Happy New Years, Mama. How are you? I will not be home today, because I have a very important meeting to attend."

"That's great honey, but the next time you sleep in the guest room, make sure you pick up your dirty clothes off the floor," The mother stated. "I found a pair of your underwear lying on the floor and I placed it in the laundry hamper. Now you know a lady is always supposed to keep those things to herself, not lying around for someone to see them."

"Mama, those aren't mine. I only wear under garments five days out of the month, and this past weekend wasn't my time to wear them," the girl said, sounding very convincing.

Gail breathes deeply before replying. "Well, they aren't mine, either. Maybe you left them here a few months prior. They belong to someone." The mother disconnected the telephone call after saying goodbye and wheeled herself to the dining room window.

Gail sat there and thought about the underwear that was found in the guest room. As she continued to think, she heard a voice come from the computer that said, "You got mail!"

"Uh, that's strange. I don't know how to use this high tech equipment," she uttered.

So Gail went to the computer and began tapping the keys to read the messages. But to her surprise, she saw where someone had been chatting online and disclosing intimate sexual secrets. She also saw illicit nude pictures of college-aged looking girls that were taken in her home. Gail mumbled angrily and said that she was going to call her daughter and get to the bottom of this.

But before she could call her daughter, Gaylin raced furiously inside the house, clothes bloody, with sweat falling from his face.

"Honey, What happened to you?"

He ignored her, pushing her wheelchair out of his way and running upstairs.

"Gaylin! What's wrong!" She shouted, wheeling herself towards the stairs, staring up with tearful eyes.

Gaylin madly storms downstairs with a loaded handgun in his hand. He opens the door and runs out into the daylight. *Bang! Bang!* Gunfire is heard and then a lady shouts out, very terror-stricken.

Eight:
Trust Me Not

Gail grabs her heart in shock as she wheels herself to the window to see what is going on. She views her husband standing out on their manicured front lawn, arguing and pointing a gun at a man's head. Police sirens are heard from afar.

"Man, don't play me like a sucker! I'll blow your mother freaking head off!" Gaylin shouted, waving the gun at the man's head that is shivering with chills, almost frightened to death.

"I don't want this gold-digging fat tramp! I banged her on last week at the motel and it wasn't all that," Gaylin said, looking at the oversized woman in disgust.

"Now, get your punk butt out of my yard and take this big ox with you before the cops come! If I hear one word you've said to the police, I'm coming after you and this time, you won't live to tell it." Gaylin demanded, shoving the gun into his pocket.

The lady and the man rush to get inside their white Ford Explorer that is parked in front of Gaylin's extravagant home. Police cars race in the driveway with neighbors shockingly looking on. The Ford Explorer speeds off quickly and Gaylin runs into the house, takes off the bloody shirt and hides the gun in the refrigerator.

Knock, knock!

"Don't you say a word about what you saw, you got it?!" Gaylin said to Gail while they stare at the closed front door.

Knock, knock!

"Yes. Who is it?" Gaylin asked angrily with his gruff voice.

"Sir, open up. It's the police!"

"Yeah. What do you want?"

"We received a call that there were gun shots being fired in the area," one officer said.

Gaylin walks over and opens the door boldly with a smirk on his face.

"Come on in, officers."

The officers walk into the neatly kept house and glance around with hands on their hips. One officer takes a seat on the couch while the other two stand up with hands folded across their chests.

"Can you all get to the point, because I don't have all day," Gaylin said, with his hands folded across his chest.

"Sir, we would like to ask you a few questions. We received a call from a distraught neighbor that you shot a man just a few minutes ago, right in your front yard. Is that true, sir?"

Gaylin laughed aloud before responding. "Heck no! Do I look like I just shot someone? Where's the body?" He sarcastically runs back to the front door and opens it. "Do you see a dead body lying in my front yard? "I just came in from a New Year's Eve celebration. The neighbors must be blind or have me mixed up with someone else."

"Sir, do you mind if we search your house?"

"Not without a search warrant. I have rights, too. Now if you don't get out of my house harassing me, I'm going to take this up with my lawyer. The local news love to report stories about bad cops," Gaylin said fiercely.

The officers look deeply at one another, one scratching the side of his neck. Gail gazes at her husband in disbelief.

"You folks have a good day. Sorry to had bothered you." The three men stroll out of the house without looking back. Gaylin peeps out the window and watches the cops drive away.

"Ooh wee! That was close!" Gaylin said, nervously walking around in the living room rubbing his hands together.

"You have five minutes to tell me what the heck is going on. I saw the whole thing! You almost shot a man over some woman!" Gail said angrily, rolling her wheelchair in his direction.

"Woman, not now!" He waves her off.

"Yes, right now! What on earth have gotten into you? I should call those cops back and tell them the whole story."

Gaylin madly stomped over near her and back slapped her in the face with his hand. The wheelchair tumbled over from the hard force. Gail fearfully lies on the cold floor, holding her pregnant stomach as Gaylin kicks her constantly in the side with his foot.

"Don't play games with me! I should bust you in the freaking mouth!" He shouts over and over again, as he kicks her like she is a piece of trash on the ground.

Gail looks up in sadness, crying for him to stop before she loses the baby. Gaylin sees the pain in her eyes. He suddenly snaps back into reality, stands still for a brief moment and helps her back into the wheelchair.

"I'm sorry, baby. I don't know what came over me."

Gail sits silently, wiping the tears from her face.

"Are you okay? Are you hungry?" He said, wiping the tears from her red eyes with his fingertip.

"Yes, but I'll be fine. I just want to be left alone," she said softly.

"Okay. Well, I'm going to get cleaned up and head over to Roscoe's. I'll let you get some rest. Do you want me to put you to bed?" He said with concern.

"No, you didn't think enough of me to come home last night. I slept the whole night in this raggedy chair. I haven't eaten nor have I taken a bath," she said, as she looks away.

"Woman, I said that I was sorry! What more you want me to do?"

"Don't worry about it. I'll call my mother and ask her to come over and bathe me," Gail said sadly, wheeling herself into their bedroom.

Dion and Roscoe Miller were sitting on their sofa at home eating buttered popcorn and drinking cold beer, watching a New Year's Day television program when someone bangs on their front door as if it was a serious emergency rudely interrupts them. Roscoe stands up and walks towards the door and Gaylin rushes in without being asked to come inside.

"Don't walk up in my house uninvited! You don't pay the bills around here!" Dion snapped, adjusting her pink robe that was slightly exposing her bra.

"He's here to see me, baby. We have some important business to discuss," Roscoe said.

"Shouldn't he be home with his wife, celebrating the New Year? Gail needs him now more than ever," Dion said with a stern look.

"Gaylin has his life to live, too. He can't be tied down taking care of her. She should be in one of those nursing homes like your Aunt Fannie," Roscoe said, smiling back at Gaylin.

"Yelp that's right. Gail should be in a nursing home. I'm getting tired of fooling around with her. She's pregnant and really getting to be a pain in the butt. All she does every day is read the Bible and talk to church folks on the phone. I can't deal with it anymore! I want out!" Gaylin said in a hostile tone.

He and Roscoe laughed like two teenage boys and walked out of the house onto the front lawn. Dion stopped the front door before it closed and angrily shouted out to Gaylin, who was lustfully looking at a neatly-figured woman getting into a silver Mercury Mountaineer with a man.

"Gail is your wife! Those vows meant for better or worse!" She slammed the door shut and sauntered off to the master bedroom.

Gaylin pumped his fist and uttered to Roscoe, "Why is she always up in my business? She needs to learn how to stay out of grown people's affairs before someone gets hurt!"

"Yeah, my wife is very nosy and can't seem to let things go. I've told her a million times to leave you alone."

"Man, enough about Dion. I have some serious issues at home. Gail is really beginning to be a headache. The other day she accused me of cheating. I felt like punching her right in the mouth," he said as he eyed Roscoe.

"You are cheating. Are you upset because she is on to you?" Roscoe replied with a giggle.

"No, I don't give a crap if she knows. But I will not have her questioning me. I'm a grown behind man who don't need a nagging wife telling me what to do or say."

"Well, you know what to do to keep her in line. Maybe you should slap her around a time or two. She'll listen then," Roscoe murmured softly.

"I have something better. I've been thinking about my future and Gail is truly in the way. She is an old nag who needs to be dumped in the ground," Gaylin mischievously said. "I mean dumped in the ground."

"I know what you mean. I love a hot, tender young thing myself. If it weren't for Dion's big paycheck at that law firm and her part time job at the office, my girlfriend's college expenses wouldn't get paid," Roscoe said, flashing all buttered teeth.

"How did we end up like this?" Gaylin frowned. "We have beautiful women on the outside and old hags on the inside."

"Well, Dion still has it going on. She is sexy, beautiful, and is too good in the bedroom. I just love a little extra meat on the side," Roscoe laughed.

"Yeah, Dion is fine, but I don't like her. She is always in my business," Gaylin sighed as he rubbed his wavy hair.

Gaylin's cell phone began ringing and it was Gail. She wanted him to come home and clean her up so that she will be dressed when Saddie and Nadine came over. Gaylin was furious and he immediately disconnected the telephone call.

"I'm tired of this! I'm tired of cleaning mess from her butt and bathing her every day! This is getting to be a little too much!" He yelled in frustration.

"Man, you got your hands full. Have you thought about hiring a nurse?"

"A nurse? That will cost extra money. My premium on my health insurance is already sky high. I have to do my best to make ends meet."

"That's why my wife is working two jobs. Someone has to bring home the bacon, because I'm disabled," Roscoe commented, sneering at himself.

"Man, your lazy behind isn't disabled. You're cheating Uncle Sam out of five hundred dollars a month," Gaylin laughed.

"You're right, and I'm going to keep taking his money because he owes me. It's only back pay for what belongs to me. I'm a disabled Veteran."

"See what I'm saying. If we had extra money we could be living the good life. I thought of a way to make some quick cash," Gaylin spoke, gazing back at Roscoe's house.

"Oh, yeah, how will you get more money? Are you planning to rob a bank?"

Gaylin looked over his shoulders and whispered, "It could bring us a million dollars. I have it all planned splendidly."

"A million dollars? What kind of work do you have in mind?" Roscoe questioned with a puzzled look, hands in his pockets.

"Getting rid of Gail for good, I found out that her dead uncle left her three million dollars and a beach home in California. She's had the money for some time now and is planning on starting some Christian film company one day."

"What? Gail has that kind of money lying around? Dion never told me anything about it."

"Gail hasn't told anyone about it, not even me. See, I overheard her and her mama talking on the phone about a lump sum of three million dollars that her great uncle Eddie Willis left before he died back in 1994."

"Really? Wow!"

"Yeah, Roscoe, the man was wealthy. He sold real estate and owned a few gas stations up north. Gail was his favorite, and since he was a widow without kids and close family members, the old coon willed everything to Gail and her country butt mama."

"That's great! If that's the case, why didn't Gail use some of that money for her surgery to walk again?" Roscoe questioned, staring at Gaylin in the face.

"I don't know, man. She's up to something. I think she wants to give it all to the church or probably to those hungry children over there in Africa. I'm getting that money and I need your help to kill her."

"Negro, are you crazy? I'm not going to prison for murder! You tried to kill her once and you didn't succeed! I don't want to get back involved!" Roscoe shouted in shock.

"No one will find out. We could make it appear again as another accident. I need for you to help me with this."

"Man, you've lost your freaking mind! You need to go to church and repent for that sin! I'm not going to help you commit murder! I think you should let it go! You have hurt

Gail already! She's crippled in a wheelchair because you hired someone to tamper with her brakes! Let it go, man! Let it go!" Roscoe pleaded and shook his head in disbelief.

Gaylin continued to try and convince Roscoe to go along with another evil plot to kill his wife. Their mouth dropped opened and eyes surprisingly bucked out like a startled deer in front of headlights as the conversation suddenly ended when they saw Dion standing close by in the yard looking at the two.

Nine:
Tragedy of Deception: Uncovered Truth

Dion gazed at the two men in disbelief as Gaylin takes a deep breath and tries to compose himself while his pounding heart beats uncontrollably with fear.

"Oh, baby, how long have you been standing there?" Roscoe said very nervously, glimpsing at Gaylin from the corner of his eye.

"Long enough to tell you to come and get this phone, I'm nobody's secretary today," She snapped, waving the cordless telephone at Roscoe who looks over a Gaylin with a sense of relief.

"You go ahead, man. I'll check you later. He waves Roscoe off. I got some things to do around the house." Gaylin marches quickly away from the house and jumps into his sporty black Corvette and speeds off. *Ooh we, that was close,* he thought.

Today seems like the longest day in history, as the New Millennium is slowly coming to an end. Gail sits back in her wheelchair listening to gospel music and enjoying her time alone with God. She rubs her pregnant belly and wishes the best for her unborn child. While in such deep thought, it was interrupted with someone ringing the front doorbell. She confusedly glances down at her watch that read six o'clock and wheeled herself to the closed door.

"Yes, who is it?"

"Open up, it's Monice."

Gail takes a deep breath and suddenly feels tension in the air.

"Ah, Gaylin isn't here. Maybe you should check back later."

"Gail, open up, please. I have a surprise for you."

Gail takes another deep breath and mumbles to herself, "Lord helps me to deal with this woman because I don't have the patience today."

The door flung open, Monice and a beautiful middle age woman around the age of sixty with sandy-brown long hair, stands in the doorway, flashing all white teeth. The lady appears very nervous, holding tight to her old worn down purse. Gail stares deeply into the woman's hazel-brown eyes as if she'd seen them before.

"Are you going to keep staring at us like we're two runaway slaves from the south or are you going to invite us inside?" Monice questioned, looking serious with her hands on her hips.

"Oh, where are my manners? Come on in," Gail said, wheeling herself away from the doorway. "Gaylin should be in soon. He went over to Roscoe's."

The middle-aged lady nervously walks around in the living room, staring at pictures on the wall. She occasionally smiles at Gail who is still staring at her with a bewilder look. Monice plops down on the sofa with one leg crossed over the other.

"Gail, I would like for you to meet---"

"Not now, Monice." The old lady cuts her off in mid-sentence. "Let me enjoy my time here."

"Aunt Rita, it's been long enough. Stop running from the past. It's time to move forward." Monice jumps off the love seat and walks over to her. Gail speaks in shock.

"Aunt Rita? Is this—I mean is she-" Gail's voice cracked, staring at the woman.

"Yeah. This is your sweet mother-in-law. Aunt Rita, this is Gaylin's wife, Gail Harris," Monice said, guiding the woman towards Gail.

"Glad to meet you, darling." Ms. Rita extends her hand to Gail in greeting.

Gail's mouth slightly opens in shock. She then extends her hand in greeting, as the two smiles gloriously at one another.

"Where have you been all these years? Gaylin told me that his mother was dead, so did you, Monice?" She starts feeling a bit deceived.

"I'm sorry, Gail, but it's a long story. Aunt Rita is here to put the past all behind her. She's here to make up for old time sake."

While the ladies all conversed, laughing, talking, and even looking at the family photo albums, Gaylin struts cheerfully in the house, humming a tone to a rap song he just heard in his car. But, when his stun struck eyes caught a glimpse to who was sitting on his living room couch as if she owns the entire world, his lovely mood suddenly changed to a deranged, over bearing, hell-born creature that the demons themselves wouldn't go up against.

"Hey, baby. I'm glad you're home," Gail said, wheeling herself to her husband, whom walks right pass her and closer to his mother who keeps her head bowed down in shame.

"Honey, look who's here to see us," Gail said, wheeling herself again towards her husband.

He keeps quiet, gawks at his mother with a silly gaze. Monice feels the tension in the air, so she quickly intervenes.

"Aunt Rita, I think it's time for us to go."

"No, she's not going anywhere!" He snapped, evilly staring at her.

"Baby, what's the matter? Aren't you happy to see your mother? It's been a long time," Gail said.

"Monice, take Gail to the shopping mall or somewhere," Gaylin said with a stern look.

"But sweetheart, we have a guest. It would be quite rude to leave your mother at a time like this. I was just getting to know her."

"Gail, take your narrow behind with Monice! Me and mama dearest have some unfinished business to discuss, right, Mom?" He sarcastically stated eyes beamed at her in hatred.

Monice unhappily wheeled Gail to her Ford Mustang and prayed silently for all damaged wounds to be healed between her cousin and his mother. Gaylin peered out the blinds and watched the car sped off. He then stomped over to his mother who had tears flowing down her face.

"I thought I told you that I never wanted to see you again!"

"Son, let me explain."

"No, Mama! You're dead to me! You're as dead as a mummy in the grave!"

"Son, please. I love you. I never stopped loving you."

"Bull crap, Mama! You only cared about pleasing my no good for nothing daddy!" I hope that son of a gun is rotting in hell!"

"Boy, don't talk like that about your father!" She slaps him in the face with an open hand. "Your father was a good man who loved his family."

"That's a bunch of horse mess, Mama! Daddy didn't care about nobody. All he cared about was money and that thing between his legs."

"Boy, I said don't talk like that about your father!" She attempted to slap him again in the face with an open hand, but he caught her hand before it reached his face and he shoved it back.

"Old woman, don't you ever touch me again! Don't ever put your slimy hands on me again!"

The mother sorrowfully walks toward the front door and attempts to open it. Gaylin forcefully blocks her path with his one hundred and ninety pound body frame.

"Oh no you're not! You're not going anywhere until I give you a piece of my mind!"

"Son, why can't you forgive me? I birth you in this world."

"So what? A big mistake that was! Don't you know that Daddy shattered my life and you stood back and done nothing? How could you? You said you loved the family? If that's true, then why on earth did you allow Daddy to die the way he did?"

"Son, I had nothing to do with that."

"Bull crap, Mama! You had all the right!"

"Son, you don't understand. That was a long time ago. Let God take control."

"Let God take control? Where was God when Daddy was mistreating the family, huh?"

The lady woefully walks around in the house, fidgeting in her skirt pocket, while Gaylin strolls behind her, chastising her as if she was a rebellious child.

"Answer me, Mama! Where was God?"

"Baby, God is everywhere. He hears and knows everything that we do. Don't be mad at God for your father's wrong doings. God loves us all and would never do anything to hurt us. Why don't we go to church on Sunday and give thanks for a new beginning?" She said, while attempting to give him a motherly hug.

"I said, don't you ever touch me!" He moves back. "I will never step a foot back in a church house as long as I live. I don't want the funeral hearse to drive my dead body to the church, take me on to the cemetery."

"Son, are you listening to yourself? What has gotten into you? You use to love church, always singing in the choir and acting in Christmas plays. I always knew you had great talent."

"Yeah, Mama, that was the old me, before I really knew the real deal about church folk."

"Son, you can't blame the church for your daddy's wrong doings. You should get on your knees and ask God for forgiveness. You have a chip on your shoulder that should not be there."

"Mama, why? Why did he do it?"

"Son, Only God knows."

"Bull crap! You knew exactly why he did it! You need to ask God to save your soul because you are not being honest with yourself!"

The mother gloomily strolls to the sofa and kneels her head downward as the tears flow down her face.

"I found Daddy, Mama. How do you think a twelve-year-old boy should feel, watching his daddy die in the church house with his pants down? Yeah, Mama, his pants down! He was in his office screwing one of the members that he just baptized and you want me to be honorable to a building that is full of hoe mongers."

The mother heart-brokenly covers her ears with her hands. "Son, I don't want to hear it!"

"Yes, you will hear it!" He forcefully pulls her hands down from her ears.

"Daddy called himself a pastor on Sunday mornings, jumping up in the pulpit praising God. I didn't understand it then, but I saw Daddy on several occasions with different church ladies on the top of his desk, their legs stretched wide open, Daddy bumping and grinding!"

The mother pretends not to listen as the tears flow harder down her face.

"Yeah, Mama! You knew about it! You knew all about his late night creeping! I admired Daddy!"

"Son, after what your father has done, he still never stopped loving his family."

"Bull crap, Mama! That's not love! He pretended to love God, but he used the church house like some cheap motel room! How could he?"

"Baby, your father had an addiction. He loved God and his family."

Gaylin then looked at her smack dab in the face. "That's a bunch of horse mess and you know it! Daddy brought women to our home night after night! You stood by and done nothing! I watched him violate our home. He didn't care, not one bit! That's why I'm the man I am today!"

The mother sobbed as she listens to her son.

"Yeah, Mama! I sleep around with different women, right under my handicapped wife's nose! She's a darn good woman, but I'm too stubborn with rage to accept it! She loves me dearly, but I have so much anger in my heart that I won't allow myself to love what's good! I love evil! Evil gives me pleasure to stay in control!"

"Son, ask God for forgiveness. It's not too late. He can help you to overcome this horrible past that has shattered your life."

"I am who I am, thanks to Daddy! See, my love for the church left when I saw Daddy lying there on the church floor, stiff dead with his manhood standing straight in the air. Sister Beverly didn't have the decency or guts to call the ambulance to get him some help. She just walked out, as if nothing happened. I guess she knew that screwing a pastor to death in the church house would make national headlines."

"Baby, take your burdens to the Lord in prayer. Don't let another day pass with this madness in your heart. You have a beautiful wife who is expecting your child. Learn to love her, son, love her."

"Mama, how can I love a woman who I truly hate? There's no love for her! I am who I am, and there's no turning back."

Midnight Creeping, Early Morning Reaping

Part 2

Burning In the Bed of Lust

Midnight Creeping, Early Morning Reaping

Ten:
Drunk as a Skunk

Dion is jerked awake in bed when Roscoe came home late one night, angry, smelling like an old wino when he began throwing things down on the floor and shouting uncontrollably like a deranged crack head who just got a quick fix.

"Get out of my house!" Roscoe shouted, trying to pull Dion out of bed by her feet.

"Take your hands off me, Roscoe! I'm calling the cops if you don't leave, right now!"

"Where's your purse? I need twenty dollars!" He said, running around the bedroom, fumbling through the closet, throwing out clothes on the floor and yelling profanity.

Dion storms out of bed and confronts Roscoe, who is going through her wallet.

"Man, if you take one cent from me, you'll be sleeping in the funeral home tonight!"

Roscoe pulled out a fifty-dollar bill from her purse and shoved it deeply into his pocket. Dion sucker punches him in the face with her fist.

"Negro, put my money back! Put my money back or the grave you shall see!" She punches him again.

"You hit me! Woman, no slut puts their hands on me!" Roscoe shouted after striking her hard in the nose. Blood gushes down her face. He then darts out of the bedroom, out of the house and jumps into his old, rundown pickup truck and speeds off.

Later that day, Saddie and Nadine arrived at the home after hearing about Dion and Roscoe's quarrel from gossiping people at the local neighborhood grocery market.

"Girl, we had to come right over after we heard about Roscoe beating you almost to death with a wooden chair," Saddie said, rushing in the house looking serious as she smacks on mint chewing gum.

"Beat me with a chair? Where did you hear that? That's a bold face lie."

"Girl, it's all over the market that Roscoe stole your money and then almost beat you to death. Your next-door neighbor, nosy Mrs. Greer, is telling everybody."

"That woman needs to mind her own business. You can't believe everything you hear. Roscoe and I just had a little fight."

"Yeah, that's what all battered women say," Saddie said, as she takes a seat on the sofa, while Nadine walks in behind her.

"I'm so glad to have friends like you all who care a lot about me," Dion said happily.

"Girl, there's nothing to it. If we were in your shoes, I'm quite sure you'll do the same for us," Saddie replied, while still smacking on mint chewing gum with one leg crossed over the other.

Dion and her friends sit in front of the television watching a program before Roscoe, who is staggering in the house from side to side smelling like an empty liquor bottle, rudely interrupts them.

"My goodness, it's not even the weekend and you're already sloppy drunk," Saddie said in laughter.

"Who sprayed on perfume?" Nadine replied while holding her nose in disgust.

"That's Roscoe smelling like a drunken skunk. He got to rise up out of my house stinking up everything." Dion demanded, as she gets up and walks towards Roscoe.

"Roscoe, where is my money?" I want my money!"

"What money?"

"My money fool!"

"Woman, get out my face and out of my house and take those two witches with you!"

Saddie and Nadine shockingly look at one another with an open mouth.

"Who you calling a witch? You fart smelling rotten-tooth sucker!" Saddie said in anger, ready to start a fight as she storms near Roscoe with a balled fist.

"You all can find your way out of my house!" Roscoe yelled, as he opens the refrigerator and grabs a beer. "I don't owe any of you heifers anything!"

Dion immediately said with both hands on her nicely firm hips, "You're not out of hot water yet. I still remember what you done to me. If I were you, I'll sleep with one eye opened, and the other eye partially opened."

Roscoe staggered back onto the porch and closed the door behind him. Saddie peeped out the window, before making a comment.

"If I were you, I'll lay Roscoe's behind out! He comes in here calling us witches! He must don't know who I am! I will mop the floor with his tongue!" Saddie said with a balled fist.

"He has the audacity to come back home as if nothing happened. I am seeking the ultimate revenge that would put him away for eternity," Dion evilly said.

"That's the way, girl," Saddie happily said as her and Dion give each other a high five.

Nadine looks at them in disbelief. She intervenes quickly with words of concern before the situation grows worse.

"It's not worth it. Let it go and let God have His way. Don't sell your soul to the devil. I know that it's hard to turn the other cheek when someone is constantly slapping you on the other, but you must be strong and allow God to fight your battles."

"I'll fight my own battles with a gun in my right hand! Roscoe is not getting away with hurting me! I'll think about my soul once Roscoe is dead and buried!"

"Roscoe is not worth the bullet in your gun. Just move out of the home and let God handle his transgressions. You can file for a divorce and collect alimony," Nadine said.

"You can't collect alimony from a deadbeat man! If anything, he'll try to get money from me!" Dion shouted. "I'm not having that!"

"I knew all the while that Roscoe was no good. A lazy man that sits on his butt and collects money from the government is a poor excuse for a man. That's why I'm marrying a man with a job. I don't care if he's flipping burgers, but as long as its honest money, then we can talk," Saddie stated in confidence.

"Enough about Roscoe, my soaps are about to come on and I can't miss it. I got to see what Samantha and Lena are up to today. Those girls always get into trouble. I need their advice on how to get even with a cheating mate."

"Girl, all you need to do is take notes from Pamela Smith on "Scald Him and Then Maul Him". I just love that show. Men would straighten up if they watched that series."

"Saddie, I love that show, too. There's nothing more exciting than watching hot grease sizzle, especially if it's being tossed on low down creeps like Roscoe."

"I'll drink to that." Saddie jokingly raises an imaginary glass to Dion. The women laughed and conversed for hours with sweet thoughts embedded inside.

Eleven:
Black Roses

June 2001 sprung in like a mighty wind, full of misfortunes and mishaps for Gail, who is celebrating her son, Jamal, with his first birthday party. She too, is celebrating her fortieth birthday with family and friends surrounding. The living room is nicely decorated with warm-colored party balloons, setting the evening off in a most joyous way. The pleasant squeals and gurgle sounds of playful, energetic toddlers aroused Jamal's bitter mood. He had been crying because he misses his father, who left the home before daybreak and hasn't returned.

Gaylin was out and about in his stylish Corvette, tucked away with his lover in front of an unkempt, rancid smelling, country setting motel room.

Gaylin said to the beautiful woman who is laying her head in his lap inside the two-seated sporty Corvette.

"Baby, I plan to buy a home in Nashville within six months. This will be our secret hang out whenever we need to get out of this city."

"Oh, that's great. I've always wanted to go to the mountains. We can spend our Christmas holiday there; snuggling in front of the fireplace, exchanging sweet kisses, and making passionate love all throughout the night."

"Well, I better get started on finalizing this deal so that everything will be ready next Christmas. I want to spend every moment with you," he said, massaging her soft, smooth skin with his fingertips.

"I always knew that you were the perfect man. It's a shame that you had to be tied down with Gail. It's only a matter of time when you will be all mine."

Gaylin rears back in the seat and looks at the woman smack dab in the face.

"What do you mean, *in a matter of time?* I hope you don't go running off your big mouth about us! I can't afford to lose my wife now! If Gail finds out about us, all hell could break loose! That is something we both will have to carry to the grave!"

"No, I won't accept that." She utters, looking away with tearful eyes. "Gail has to know how we both feel towards one another. This secret is terrorizing my life. I can't live without you. She will understand that you never loved her and you no longer want to be with her."

"Are you nuts? I'm not fixing to leave my wife over you! I have too much invested in her! Gail is my one-way meal ticket back to Hollywood!" He shouted his tone very hostile.

"So, I'm not good enough to marry, but good enough to screw, huh?" She said, staring at him with pain of dissent in her eyes.

Gaylin sits silently with his hands resting in his lap.

"Answer me! So...I'm good enough to screw when your horny butt wants a good piece for the night, right?"

Gaylin turns his blank expression towards the woman and lets out a gust of air.

"I really don't think I owe you an explanation."

"Am I just sex to you, Gaylin? I thought you loved me! I've sacrificed a lot to be with your sorry butt! Not anymore! I'm going to tell Gail everything!"

She opens the unlocked door and quickly jumps out of the car, racing towards the highway. Gaylin gets out and runs behind her, trying to salvage the relationship before things get out of hand.

"I'm sorry! Come back! I do love you!"

She stops dead in her tracks along the side of the road with traffic going in both directions. Gaylin catches up with her and slowly grabs her from behind.

"I'm sorry. I never meant to hurt you. Let's go on back to the room and let me show you how much you mean to me." He then places a soft, sensuous kiss on her lips.

While they both were walking back towards the tacky-looking motel, his cell phone starts to ring. He retrieves the cell phone from inside his pocket and looks at the caller ID with a bewilder gaze.

"Gosh, I wonder who that could be?" He continues to stare at the unknown number on his cell phone.

Ring, ring, ring, ring. He continues to look at the cell phone.

"Aren't you going to answer it? It could be important," The lady said, looking over at the cell phone.

"Hello," he said, hesitantly.

"Gaylin, we're all waiting on you. Jamal is ready to open his birthday presents," Gail said.

"That's not my problem. I'm busy right now." *Click.* He disconnects his cell phone and continues to walk back to the motel with his lover.

Several hours had passed and Nadine, Saddie and Mrs. Bradford were cleaning up after the birthday party. Jamal had fallen asleep on Gail's lap, with dried tear crust on his face. Saddie had bad thoughts to herself about Gaylin and was wondering why he missed another important time in his wife's life.

"I wonder why Gaylin isn't here to celebrate his son's first birthday," Nadine suddenly said while sweeping potato chip crumbs off the kitchen floor.

"Where is Gaylin? I know he isn't at work. It's almost after six o'clock," Saddie then said, glancing down at her watch.

"I think he had to work late today. Give him some time, he'll be here," Gail said, while she holds Jamal closely to her bosom."

There is a hard knock at the front door that startles everyone. Mrs. Bradford nervously gets up from her seat and meets a sumo wrestler looking white woman standing in the doorway holding a bouquet of black roses and one red rose.

"Hello, Is this Gail Harris' residence?"

"Yes, it is. How can I help you?" Mrs. Bradford said, looking puzzled at the bouquet of black roses.

"I have a special birthday delivery for her," the florist said, handing the roses to Mrs. Bradford, who has an incredulous look on her face. She closes the door and hesitantly places the roses on an end table in the living room.

Saddie gasped and yelled, looked serious "Black roses! What kind of joke is this?"

"Honey, who sent you these roses?" Mrs. Bradford said with a caring tone. "These look like dead funeral home flowers."

"I don't know, Mama. Open the card and see who sent it. Maybe the florist delivered the wrong flowers."

Mrs. Bradford opens the tightly sealed card that is covered with musty scent of body odor. Gail, Saddie and Nadine attentively sit closely and listen to the words that read: *Happy fortieth birthday. Roses are red, but these dozens are black. Your husband is with me now, stroking me down in our love shack. Roses are red, and your husband's love for you is dead. Just a reminder to tell you that he is so good in the bed.*

Mrs. Bradford heartbrokenly drops the card on the floor.

Saddie madly picks the card up off the floor and shouts with spit flying from her mouth. "What slut sent this card?" I'm going to beat the slut!"

"Don't use degrading terms like that. It's not Christian like to curse and use bad words," Nadine said, still upset about the card.

"That's right. Don't use that nasty talk in here," Mrs. Bradford said while walking towards Gail who has tears in her eyes.

"Well, excuse my French. I apologize, but some hooker sent this horrible card to Gail and I'm upset about it. Some gold-digger is after her husband and we're not going to let it happen," Saddie said arrogantly, massaging Gail's back. Gail has tears flowing down her face.

"Lord have mercy! Lord have mercy!" Mrs. Bradford cried out, hands extended to the Heavens. "The devil is busy! Get that mess out of this house!" Nadine quickly grabs the flowers and disposes them outside in the trash dumpster.

Gaylin later strutted into the house wearing an iron-crisp pair of jeans with a pull-over name brand tee-shirt. He walks over to his wife, who is joyfully playing with their son, who has awakened from his tiresome sleep. Gaylin places a warm kiss on her lips that left a sweet fruity scent, like flavored lip-gloss.

"What's that smell? Have you been eating strawberries?" Gail questioned, licking her lips. "Your lips are greasy with the scent of something sweet."

"Strawberries? No, it could be you," he said, wiping his lips with the back of his hand.

"Yeah, he's been eating strawberries, alright," Saddie sarcastically said, looking dead in his eyes.

"Stop causing trouble. I think we should leave now and give them some privacy," Nadine whispered in Saddie's ear.

"I guess I'll be going, too. I'm going to brunch in the morning," Mrs. Bradford said, while gathering her belongings.

When the house was totally empty from party guests, Gail wheeled herself over to her husband who is laughing and rolling around on the floor with Jamal.

"Where were you today? This was Jamal's first birthday and you didn't think enough of him to spend time with him."

Gaylin ignored her and continued playing with his baby boy, who was releasing a toothless smile at him.

"Answer me! You should have been here with us!" She shouted.

"Where do you get off telling me where to go? I'm a grown behind man who don't have to report to you! Now get off my back!" He shouted, still rolling on the floor with the baby.

Gail snapped back, "I'm tired of you acting like an irresponsible teenage boy! You have responsibilities! I can't do it alone! I need help!"

Gaylin immediately stood up from off the floor, eyes stretched as wide as they could. He angrily grabbed Gail by the collar of her blouse.

"You're not my problem! I don't have to do nothing but stay black and die! I told you at the beginning that I didn't want this baby! So you deal with him!"

He races out of the living room into the den. Gail wheels herself behind him, leaving Jamal on the floor crying.

"I thought this baby brought joy to your life! I thought that you were happy!" Gail sobbed in tears.

"I haven't been happy in a long time! Maybe I got married for all the wrong reasons!" He said. "I think it was a mistake."

"Oh, you wait almost twenty-one years and two children to tell me that our marriage was a mistake! You got one helleva nerve!" Gail shouted, the baby crying tremendously in the living room.

Gaylin quickly regains composer and calmly speaks to his wife who is highly upset, shivering in the wheelchair.

"If you want to go, then go. I don't need you. I can do bad by myself," She said in a soft tone. Gail then wheels herself back into the room and comforts her baby.

"I didn't mean it like that. What I'm saying is that I've been unhappy with our situation. Lately, I've been working long hours and haven't spent time with you. I'm going to do better and show you how much my family means to me," he said, as he reaches for the crying baby.

Twelve:
Secrets of Burning Desires

Gaylin tosses and turns in his sleep, slowly mumbling out familiar names while Gail sleeps peacefully beside him in their king size bed. An annoying vibrating sound, coming from Gaylin's pajama pants, awakes his wife at three o'clock in the morning. Gail, who is lying down on her left side reaches deeply into her husband's pocket and discovers that he has a secret cell phone that she knows nothing about. The cell phone vibrates again, and an unknown number flashes on the caller ID.

He is in such a deep sleep, snoring and slobbering out the mouth until he didn't feel the phone vibrating against his skin. Gail immediately answers the call quietly underneath her bed sheets.

"Hello," she said, speaking softly into the mouthpiece.

"May I speak to Gaylin?"

"He's asleep. May I ask whose calling?"

"It's CeCe."

"CeCe who?" Gail is puzzled, peeping from underneath the sheets over at her sleeping husband.

The woman begins to get impatient and she yells in frustration.

"Is this his mother? Why are you screening his calls? Let me speak to Gaylin!"

Gail's eyebrows rise in anger and she clears her throat before speaking.

"No, I'm not his mother! I'm his wife and don't you call my house, again!" *Click.* She disconnects the cell phone and angrily throws it against the wall. Gaylin awakes startles and jumps up in bed from the loud noise.

"What was that?" He said, staring at Gail who is pretending to be asleep.

Early morning sunshine welcomes Gaylin, who rises out of bed and sluggishly walks into the bathroom, slips off his pajamas and steps his caramel muscular body into his shower before rushing off to his high-maintenance office job. Gail still lies in bed, sadly listening to her baby boy play in his crib, but she is unable to get out of bed to go and take care of him.

Gaylin has showered, shaved, eaten breakfast and is decked out GQ-style. He notices that his cell phone is lying flat on the floor near the bedroom entrance. *"I wonder how this got here?* " He thought, while reaching to pick up the cell phone.

"Baby, I'm on my way to work," Gaylin said to his wife who is still lying in bed.

"Okay. Make sure the door is unlocked so that Mama has a way to get in," she said bitterly, with bad thoughts about the secret cell phone in her head.

As Gaylin attempts to walk out of the house, Gail shouts to him.

"Who is CeCe?!"

Gaylin stops dead in his tracks and strolls back to the bedroom with a smug look on his face.

"Why you asked that?"

"Because she called your little secret cell phone at three in the morning," She replied back, voice trembling.

"I don't know a CeCe. Maybe she had the wrong number," he said nonchalantly as he storms out of the house."

Mrs. Bradford had come over later that morning to get Gail out of the bed. This was a daily routine for her mother, because her daughter truly needed the help. After the woman had bathed Gail and cooked breakfast, Jamal was in desperate need for attention.

"Mama, this is too hard for me," Gail said. "My baby cries for me, and I can't even get out of the bed to walk over to his crib and get him."

"Hush, child. Everything will be alright. Don't be hard on yourself."

"Mama, I'm crippled, stuck here in this raggedy-behind wheelchair. I can't do nothing for my son but lay him on my lap. Why me? Why me, Mama?" Gail said with eyes full of water.

"Baby, God don't make mistakes. It's a reason for you being in this wheelchair. Just take one day at a time and be blessed for life. Ask God to make you stronger and to accept the fact that you are crippled," the mother said in a caring tone.

"Mama, Gaylin doesn't love me anymore. A woman called and disrespected my house this morning. I think he's seeing someone." She lowered her voice.

"Sweetheart, trust your instincts and allow God to do the rest. It takes two to make a marriage work and it seems like you're the only one working."

Mrs. Bradford soon left the residence, leaving Gail and the baby home alone. Gail woefully listens to the world's greatest gospel song 'Oh Lord Is It Me' as her son naps on her lap. But within an hour, Saddie arrives at the house while on her two-hour teacher's planning period.

"Girl, why are you listening to that funeral home music? Saddie said, as she struts into the unlocked front door, wearing a black two-piece pants business suit."

"No time for jokes, Saddie. This is my meditation time. I love to listen to old time gospel."

"Well, I didn't mean to disturb you. I was in the area and decided to come by to pay you a visit," Saddie said. "Girl, are you okay?"

"Yeah, I'm fine."

"Stop lying. You're not okay. You've been crying, haven't you?" Saddie said, as she walks closer to Gail who is trying to hold back the tears.

"I'm worthless and a disgrace to society." Gail burst out in tears. "My husband doesn't love me anymore and I'm stuck here in this wheelchair in the prime of my life. I should be out and about enjoying myself."

"Gail, have you even thought and listened to yourself? What were you doing before I rudely interrupted you?"

Gail sits quietly, looking into a daze.

"Huh? Gail, I'm talking to you." Saddie waves her hand in Gail's face to direct her attention back to the conversation. "What were you doing before I rudely interrupted you?"

"I was meditating to God." Gail remembered.

"Yes, so you have no reason for self-pity. My grandmother use to tell me when I was a child to plead the blood of Jesus Christ whenever I'm feeling depressed."

Gail looks at Saddie, while wiping the tears as they fall with the back of her hand.

"I know that through the shed blood of Jesus Christ, God has given us supernatural victory over depression. In Romans 4:18-22, Abraham had hoped when there was no reason to hope. You should start hoping and having faith that things will get better. There's always a reason for the season," Saddie said while releasing a pearly white smile.

The cool breeze night air creeps in and the wind whistles as Gail lays slump over asleep in her wheelchair with the baby on her lap. It's half-past eleven o'clock and Gaylin is in a sleazy motel room, cuddled up with his lover in a urine smelling bed that sagged in the middle.

"I got to be going soon. I told Gail that I had to work late again, tonight."

"Before you leave, I have something that I've been dying to tell you," The woman said, smiling from ear to ear, as she strokes his bare chest with her fingertips.

"Oh, yeah. What is it?" He said with glee.

"We're going to have a baby!" She shouted, smiling up at his now frowned face.

"What? We're going to have what?" He said, looking serious as he rises off the squeaky bed.

"I'm almost eight weeks pregnant. I found out today when I went to the doctor. Isn't that good news?"

"Heck no! I'm a married man! I can't have a baby with you!" He said, while fumbling around the room for his clothes.

"Here, take this money and go find you a doctor to go get rid of this baby," he said, while handing her a few hundred-dollar bills from his wallet.

She angrily jumps up out of the bed and snatches the money out of his hand and throws it on the floor.

"You can take this money and ram it up your butt because I'm not killing my child!"

"It may not be my baby! How do I know that you're not screwing around with another married man!" Gaylin said, as he rushes to put on his pants.

"I've slept with only you and you know it!"

"I don't know that! It seems like you get around easily! I'm not claiming that baby! If Gail finds out about this, all hell could break loose!" He said while buttoning his shirt.

"I'm telling Gail everything. She needs to know about our affair." The woman said with a stern look.

Gaylin's hazel-brown eyes evilly gaze in her direction as he marches to her.

"Look! I've worked my butt off trying to satisfy you! Now, if you want to go running your big mouth, then you will have to suffer the consequences! No one short changes me and live to tell about it!" He said as he walks out the motel room and slams the door behind him.

The next day, Gaylin appears quite speechless and wants to be alone, sitting in the den watching a blank television screen. Gail is in the next room, talking and playing with her son as he sits happily on her lap. Monice comes over to the house, extremely blissful and joyous when she relates the wonderful news to everyone that she is expecting a child. A few hours later, Roscoe cheerfully storms over and reveals his good news that he and Dion are expecting a baby. All the sudden news about having a baby sends Gaylin into a state of depression.

So he decides to go outside to retrieve the mail, to get a fresh breath of clean air. But as he is walking back inside the house, he sees the most beautiful, cinnamon brown skin young teenage girl, with a head full of thick black hair, helping her father move into the vacant house next door. Gaylin's eyes look in lust and his body long for her touch. He immediately wants to throw away a good marriage, which truly doesn't mean anything to him.

Thirteen:
Sweet Temptation

Gaylin stands outside his door with a handful of mail and watches the young beautiful girl move abruptly, carrying furniture and other house hold items into their new home. The girl notices Gaylin staring at her, so she flashes a warm smile in his direction and continues to unload the truck. Gail immediately interrupts his deep fantasy with a loud shout coming from the living room. He walks back into the house and questions her about their new neighbors.

"Honey, who are those people moving next door?" Gaylin stated, eyes beaming with admiration.

"I don't know, sweetheart. But I heard that the man graduated from my alma mater," She replied, bouncing Jamal on her lap.

"I think I'll go over and offer my assistance. I did see a heavy couch that looks hard to move. I'll be back shortly," he said, brushing his wavy hair with the palm of his hand.

"Okay, the bus will be picking the baby and me up within the next fifteen minutes. I decided to go to the mall to get that latest novel while it's still on sale," Gail stated.

Gaylin kissed his wife on the forehead and then walked proudly next door to meet the new neighbors, who appeared to be very pleasant and content with themselves. When he approached their yard, he lustfully noticed that the girl was very beautiful up close. The father happily meets Gaylin at the front door. He is extremely handsome with smoky gray eyes and a slick bald head.

"Hello, may I help you?"

"Hey, I'm Gaylin Harris, your neighbor. I came over to see, did you all need help moving that heavy furniture?"

"Yes, I sure do. I could use all the help possible." The man chuckled. "Oh, by the way, I'm Frank Dehner." He extends his hand in greeting.

"Is she your wife?" Gaylin said, eyeballing the beautiful girl who is still unloading the truck. "If so, you're one very lucky man."

"No, this is my daughter. I've been divorced for almost ten years. I received custody of my daughter when I caught my wife in bed with another man. We moved from Arizona, so that she could begin college here this fall. We've been doing quite fine since I left that home wrecking ex-wife of mine."

"I know how you feel, partner. I'll leave my wife, too, if I ever caught her cheating on me. See, we as men can do what we want. We can cheat and have a little cute thing on the side if we wanted too, right?" Gaylin said while laughing.

"I disagree, totally." Frank looks at him. "Marriage is supposed to be honorable, making a commitment before God. Some people these days are just marrying for the sake of being married. Don't know or care nothing about its essence and sacredness. That's why I teach my daughter to stay away from low life creeps who only wants her for one thing. My daughter and I have a good relationship. She knows that she is beautiful and that men will try to take advantage of her."

"I know how you feel, partner, because I have a daughter that's in college and I'll break a sucker's neck if he mistreats her," Gaylin said, glancing over at the young girl.

"Chloe knows what to do if a snake comes her way," Frank said. "We're Christians and she knows that there are a lot of black snakes that are out there waiting to steal her innocence."

Gaylin thought that not only would he steal her innocence, but her heart too. She was as pure as the Virgin Mary and that excited him a great deal.

While Frank and Gaylin continued to move the heavy furniture into the well-kept house, Gail later phoned her husband on his cell.

"Hello, baby. Could you please come to the mall to pick up the baby and me?" She stated, urgency in her voice.

"No, I'm busy! Can't you catch the bus home?" Gaylin shouted into the mouthpiece.

"The bus quits carrying people on this side of town at five o'clock. I tried calling my mother, but she wasn't home," she said as the baby cries in the background.

"I told you that I'm busy! You should have stayed your butt at home! I'm not coming now!" He shouted before disconnecting the call. Frank is staring at him with a stern look.

"You don't have to finish this. It seems as though that person needs you more than I do," Frank said, while lifting a suitcase from the inside of the truck.

"No, man. I'll finish up. That was just my dumb wife trying to get a ride home from the mall," He bitterly said. "See, my wife is paralyzed and thinks that she should be treated like a baby. She needs to understand that I can't be beside her all the time."

Frank questioned in disbelief. "Paralyze? That was your wife who I saw got on that city bus with a baby?"

"Yeah, that's her. She's a strong woman, though. She'll get home safely."

"Why would you allow your handicap wife to find her way home from a busy mall with a baby? I don't think that's right, man. You go and get your wife and I'll finish moving this stuff," Frank said.

Gaylin kept refusing to go and get his wife until he heard Chloe yell to her father that she was going to the mall with a couple of friends. Gaylin immediately decided that it was his duty to go and pick up his wife from the mall. But Gail was far from his mind when he arrived at the mall's parking lot. He was thinking about the young girl and wanted an opportunity to meet her on his terms.

Within thirty minutes, Gaylin sees a mixed raced teenage boy, driving a red Cherokee jeep. He drops off three young college students along with Chloe in front of the mall's entrance. Gaylin looks in his mirror and begins brushing his soft wavy hair with the palm of his hand. He later gets out of his car and follows Chloe all through the mall. He watches her in lust as she walks with her friends, swinging her soft, head full of black hair from side to side. Suddenly Gaylin's cell phone rings and it is Gail, calling from a nearby payphone with the baby crying in the background. He ignores the call and then turns off the cell phone.

Chloe excuses herself from her friends and goes into a sports body shop, filled with energetic shoppers fumbling through the clothes for a good buy. Gaylin walks behind her, pretending to have accidentally bumped into her.

"Excuse me, ma'am, but can you help me with this?" He said, holding up a shirt he just grabbed off the hangers.

"I'm sorry, but I don't work here," Chloe said as she looks at him. "Don't I know you?"

Gaylin walks closer to her and smiles.

"You're my neighbor. What a surprise to see you here,"

Chloe smiled and said while fumbling through summer clothing.

"Yes, I love going to the mall."

Gaylin looks into her big brown eyes as she occasionally glances up at him.

"You have some pretty eyes. Have you ever thought about modeling?"

"No, I'm camera shy. I enjoy reading and staying informed about the world. I'm going to school to become a lawyer," she said happily, admiring a pink button-down blouse that she grabs off a hanger.

Gaylin attempts to make another statement until the girl excuses herself and goes back to meet her friends, who are all standing in front of the body shop engaging in conversation.

In the meantime, Gail sits in her wheelchair at the mall's side entrance as she continues to dial Gaylin's cell phone. However, one hour later, she decides to wheel herself back home with the baby on her lap. Jamal begins crying and wants to be fed. While she tiresomely struggles with the baby and watches attentively to the oncoming traffic, Frank, who is in the mist, notices her waiting at a stop sign with little help to cross the street. So he drives his black Dodge pickup truck over to the center lane and gets out to assist her.

"Hello, my name is Frank Dehner, your new neighbor! Would you like a ride home?" He shouted to her, traffic moving in both directions.

"Thank you, sir, but I'll manage!" She shouts back, still trying to cross the busy street.

Frank made his way near her and continues to offer his assistance.

"No, I'm not going to let you wheel yourself home on these busy streets. It's not safe for a woman to be out here alone. I thought your husband was coming to get you? He left my house and said that he was coming to the mall."

"He lied to you. I have been sitting there for over two hours. I tried calling his cell number and received only his mailbox."

"I was on my way home from Bible study, praising the Lord. So would you let me do my Godly duty and take you home?" He warmly smiles at her who is smiling back, from ear to ear.

"Okay, Mister. I see you're not giving up without a fight," She jokingly said.

Frank assists Gail and the baby into his truck with the wheelchair on the back. Jamal had previously stopped crying and is playing with the man, who has shown great admiration for Gail and the baby.

"I remember when Chloe was that young," Frank said, looking at Jamal who is grabbing at the stirring wheel.

"Oh, you have a daughter? How old is she?"

"She's eighteen. She'll be starting at the university this fall."

"That's great. My daughter attends the university, too. She'll be graduating soon," Gail said, feeling a bit of happiness.

They both continue to converse in sweet conversation until Frank drives up into Gail's driveway, with gospel music sounding. Gaylin had driven home earlier and now sees the black Dodge pickup truck in his driveway. He walks out into the yard and notices that it is Gail and their new neighbor, both joyfully singing the gospel song that is playing from the CD track. Gaylin walks over to the truck with frown lines all in his face.

"Your wife is something else. I think I'm going to enjoy being your neighbor!" Frank said as he takes the wheelchair off the back of the truck. Gail looks at Frank with a warm smile.

"What happened to you, man? I thought you were going to the mall to get this beautiful lady," Frank said while placing Gail in the wheelchair.

"Huh, beautiful? Man you must be blind. There's nothing beautiful about her. Not even the bottom of her feet," Gaylin chuckled, while walking away without lifting a finger to help assist Gail in the wheelchair.

She kneels, her sad face down in shame as a teardrop falls on Jamal. Frank is dismal and stands still for a brief moment. He couldn't believe that Gaylin disrespected her in that manner. He then pushes her wheelchair into the house.

"Does he always talk to you like that?" Frank asked.

"Pay Gaylin no mind, he's just being himself," she said, trying to hide her pain.

"No woman in your condition should be treated this way. As a matter of fact, no woman should be treated harshly," Frank said, wheeling Gail's wheelchair into the living room.

Gaylin overheard the conversation when he walked downstairs into the living room. Frank is standing near Gail, who has the baby laid across her lap.

"I think it's time for you to go home, partner! Get to stepping!" He said rudely with his gruff voice.

"I don't mean to cause problems, but I didn't like that statement you said to your wife outside, and I don't like the fact that you almost made her wheel herself home in a wheelchair with a baby," Frank said, staring at him smack dab in the face.

"Look, partner, this is my wife! Maybe if you had put a foot up your ex-wife's butt, she wouldn't have cheated on you! I wear the pants in this house and you wear them in yours, so you can see your way out!" He shouted with a bold voice.

Frank leaves the home with a silent prayer in his heart.

"Oh, you have eyes for that chump?" Gaylin said to his wife, who is still holding their son.

"No, He's a very nice man. I think you need to go and apologize to Frank. He is a good man who loves the Lord."

"I'm not apologizing to anyone! He crossed the line when he came in here telling me how to talk to you. No one tells me what to do, no one!" Gaylin snapped.

"Well, I'll go over and apologize for you. Frank was very kind to think of Jamal and me. You were nowhere to be found when we needed you," she said with content.

Gaylin suddenly slaps Gail in the face with the back of his hand. Blood gushes out and falls on Jamal.

"Don't you ever talk to me like that! I don't give a crap what you think about that man! If I ever see you over to his house you will regret that you ever knew me!" He shouted.

Gail then wheeled herself into the bathroom to wash her bloody nose with a cold washcloth. The next day, Roscoe invited Gaylin and Gail over for a barbeque cookout in his backyard. Gail was too tired to attend, so she decided to stay at home with the baby. Gaylin got dressed GQ-style and went over with much gossip to say to his friend, who was out in the yard with a group of men, smoking blunts and drinking beer.

"Man, it's the most finest, good-looking and sexist young thing that have moved next door to me. I want her, man. I want her real bad," Gaylin said, puffing on a thick blunt.

"Oh, yeah, what about your other women? You don't have the time to juggle another woman," Roscoe said while reaching for the blunt.

"Man, this young girl got it going on. She's special and pure, unlike those trashy-looking, saggy breast hoochies from the club. She's gorgeous with a juicy petite body," he said. "I'm not letting that fresh meat pass by."

"We can make this cookout short and make plans for tonight," Roscoe said while looking back towards his home.

"My girl, Carla, is home from college and we both can double date tonight, right?"

"Well, she doesn't know how I feel, yet. I tried to tell her at the mall, but she left before I could say something," Gaylin said shyly.

"Go and tell her. No woman can resist you. You're one of those pretty fellows that can get any woman he wants," Roscoe said, as he places a chicken leg on the grill.

"Do you have a telephone book? I'll call her and ask her to meet me at the restaurant."

"No, go on to her house and tell her. Girls like it when men show up unexpectedly to their house," Roscoe said, puffing on the thick blunt.

"But Gail is home. I can't let her see me next door," Gaylin said. "The girl's father might be home, too. I don't want any trouble."

"You can use my truck, but make sure you're back within two hours because I have to pick up Carla from off the campus," Roscoe said softly, glancing back at his house.

Gaylin runs happily in high speed to the worn-down pickup truck and goes to visit Chloe.

He later approaches the quiet neighborhood and parks Roscoe's old beat-up pickup truck down the street from his house. He boldly walks up to the girl's front door when he notices that Frank's truck wasn't there. Before he attempts to ring the doorbell, the door flung open with gospel music being heard in the background. Chloe is startled and gives him a puzzled look.

"Oh, I thought that you were my friend. I'm expecting company."

"Are you going to invite me inside? I have something important to tell you," Gaylin said, looking over her shoulders with a slight grin.

"My father doesn't allow strangers in the home when he's not here," She timidly said.

"I'm not a stranger. I live next door and I came here to apologize to Frank about the other day. I said some cruel things to him."

"Well, he's not here. He's in a church meeting and I'll give him the message," she said, attempting to close the door.

Gaylin peeked his head through the door and said, "Isn't that the greatest Sam Davis gospel song?"

"Yes, he was magnificent. His songs are so inspirational," She said with a grin.

Gaylin then made his way into the house pretending to be a music fan of Sam Davis. He walks back to her bedroom where the music is playing.

"He sounds so good. I have his CD at home," He lied, strolling around in the girl's bedroom, staring at her glamour perfect pictures on the wall.

Chloe angrily stands still in the living room and shouts to him with a bold voice.

"You can't be in my room! You have to leave before my father comes home!"

Gaylin walks out of the neatly girly bedroom with lust in his eyes. He struts near her; she is slowly walking away from him. He then closes and locks the front door.

"You're so beautiful. I want to kiss your soft creamy lips," he said with a nasty whisper.

"I'm calling my daddy if you don't get out of here," She demanded, shaking a finger at him.

Chloe attempts to runs over to the telephone, but Gaylin blocks her path with his one hundred and ninety pound body frame. He pulls her closer to him and she yanks away, running freely around in the living room.

"Get out, now, or I will scream!" She said.

He blocks her path again and holds onto her firm body tightly.

"Your skin is so soft and beautiful. I fantasize about being with you," he said, caressing her skin with his fingertips.

"You better back off and get your filthy hands off me! I'm calling my father if you touch me again!" She demanded, trying to push his hands away.

He touches her breasts that are very firm and soft, like a cotton pillow.

"Your breasts are so soft. Let me be the first to show you a good time," he said while massaging her irresistible toned skin.

"Let go of my arm! Let go of my arm you filthy animal!" She blurted out.

Gaylin forcefully throws her petite body onto the floor, rips open her blouse, pulls up her miniskirt, yanks off her bikini underwear, and then begins unzipping his pants.

Fourteen:
Playing with Fire

Gaylin pulls down his pants and spreads Chloe's legs as wide as they would go. Her heart flutters while tears stroll down her glorious face. She prays silently, as she attempts to watch her innocence being taken away.

"Don't worry, you'll enjoy this just as much as I will," Gaylin said, holding her down with his right arm, while his left hand reaches inside his boxers.

Ring, ring! A sound is coming from the front doorbell. Chloe shouts uncontrollably and Gaylin slaps her in the face with an open hand.

"Chloe, Chloe, are you okay?!" The man turns the locked door handle. "Open the door! Open this door, right now!" the guy said from the locked door, hearing her crying tremendously.

Gaylin then grabbed his pants and ran into the bathroom as if nothing happened. Chloe raced to the front door with her blouse torn opened and her underwear on the floor.

"What on earth is going on? I heard you crying and yelling when I drove up," Bryant said, as he rushes into the house looking around.

"Oh my God! I was almost raped! I was almost raped!" She hysterically said with tearful eyes, hands over her chest.

"Raped?" Bryant madly looks around the house. "Where is he now? I'm going to kill him when I get my hands on him!"

Gaylin cowardly locks the bathroom door and tries to crawl out through the window. Bryant hears the rattling noise coming from the bathroom and he races to the entrance with a balled hand and turns the doorknob that is locked. *Bang Bang.* Bryant knocks hard on the fasten door.

"I'm going to kill you! Come out, you coward or I will kick the door down!" *Bang Bang.* He kicks and knocks on the closed door.

"Just call the police. Let the authorities handle the situation," Chloe said while shivering in fear as she puts back on her clothing.

"Bring your butt out here, you punk!" Bryant shouts before he kicked open the locked door and found only shoe prints leading to an open window. He races to the window and sees Gaylin running down the street.

"Move out my way, baby!" Bryant said to Chloe as he pushes her away from the bathroom's entrance and angrily runs out the front door, chasing behind Gaylin who has already made his way back to Roscoe's pickup truck.

"Sucker!" Bryant shouts to Gaylin who speeds away in the truck, leaving burnt tire marks on the street.

Chloe attempts to call the police, but sees Gail unhappily sitting outside underneath an oak tree with the baby in her lap. She immediately places the telephone back on the receiver and walks slowly to the kitchen window and stares deeply at the woman who appears to have a million things going on in her mind. Bryant storms back inside the house in a heated rage.

"Call the police! I'm not going to let that clown run free! I'm going to whip his___"

"Just let it go!" She cuts him off in mid-sentence. "I'll let God handle it." Chloe continues to stare at Gail through the window.

"What? Are you serious? No, baby, this clown needs to be caught," he said rigorously. "I'm not going to let no man get away with putting his hands on my woman."

"Bryant, don't worry about it. Promise me that you won't tell my father about this," she said, still looking at Gail from the window.

"What? Baby, you're taking this turn the other cheek thing a little too extreme. God did give us sense," he said, looking dead into her brown eyes.

"Just drop it. I don't feel like talking about it anymore. Just promise me you won't tell my father," She demanded with an irritated look.

Chloe felt terrible that she could not reveal to her boyfriend that her next-door neighbor, Gaylin, was the attacker. She saw the pain of an unhappy woman in Gail's eyes as she held the baby underneath the oak tree in her backyard. Chloe had compassion for people and could not allow seeing Gail burden down in sorrow. So she took the issue to God in prayer and hoped that one day Gaylin Harris would pay dearly for the assault he had inflicted on her.

Gaylin finally arrived back at Roscoe's house drenched in sweat wearing a fake smile. Dion met him at the front door, gazing at him from head to toe.

"What do you want? Roscoe is busy," She speaks dryly, still standing in the doorway.

"Roscoe and I have plans for tonight. So will you tell him that I'm here?"

Roscoe steps out the door all dressed up wearing a clean pair of iron-crisp jeans, button-up black shirt and strong-scented cologne. His hair on his head and face were neatly trimmed, a perfect imitation of a movie star.

"Where do you think you're going?" Dion said to her husband while rolling her eyes.

"Out," He said nonchalantly as he struts outside to his old run down pickup truck.

Dion strolls behind him, speaking loudly so that the neighbors could hear her.

"Where are you going, smelling all good for a change? Your dumb butt needs to go and find a job!" She struts back to her porch.

As the sun diminishes into the clouds, and the smell of midnight musk will later arrive, Gail is still sitting outside in her wheelchair with the baby on her lap. She focuses her attention on Heaven, as she watches in deep thought the stars that appear from up above, and the moon circles the earth. She instantly wishes to be a total connection with such peaceful particles surrounding the land. The pleasant thoughts were interrupted with Dion blowing a loud car horn in the driveway. Gail wheels herself in the front yard.

"Your no good man is out with my husband!" Dion shouted, while getting out of the car and angrily walking towards Gail. "Yeah, I know they're up to no good!"

"They probably went out for a drink. You know how men are when they get together," Gail said, as she wheels herself up the wheelchair ramp into her house.

"I know. That's what I'm afraid of. I know Roscoe is up to no good. I'm going to find out what's going on. I'm not going to be played like a fool."

"Stop worrying about Roscoe. Put your trust in God and allow Him to handle the rest," Gail said while opening the door.

"Child, wake up and smell the coffee! You know and I know that those men are up to no good! I'm not going to be played like a dumb fool! I have all of Roscoe's rags in the trunk of my car! If I catch him with a stank breath heifer tonight, then his behind is grass and I'm the lawnmower!" Dion shouted while angrily walking back to her vehicle. She speeds off in her Beige Malibu and drives around in the city in search for her husband.

"So, how did things go with that young hottie?" Roscoe said to Gaylin, who is sitting up in the truck staring off gloomily in space like a lost astronaut.

"Man, did you hear me?" Roscoe said. "Hello, Gaylin. Come back to earth," he said to him, waving his hand in his face trying to get his attention.

"Oh, yeah. What did you say?" Gaylin said confusedly.

"I said how did things go with that young hottie?" He reiterates, releasing a puzzled look while driving down the highway.

"Oh, yeah, man, I'm not interested anymore." He finally snaps back into reality full of haughtiness. "She doesn't have enough booty for me and I don't like a light skin woman, face is too pale and they seem to age faster. I love myself a smooth chocolate lady."

"Really? You could have fooled me. I thought you liked anything with shaved legs," Roscoe said, flashing a wide grin.

Roscoe and Gaylin later arrived at a local restaurant, just a few miles from the university where they stopped along the way to pick up their dates, CeCe and Carla, who both reside on the college campus. Dion aggressively drives around the city, looking around in all directions for her husband's old Ford beat-up pickup truck.

People are out and about walking in and out of the restaurant. Gaylin escorts CeCe, who is wearing a long strapless dress with a slit way up her thigh. Her elegant dress attire brings much attention when she steps into the country setting restaurant where common folks are gulping down sweet tea and lemonade, smacking on fried chicken that was taken from off the buffet bar.

When Gaylin looks back near the entrance section, he sees Chloe with a young man, appearing to be around her age, standing in line waiting to come inside. She is looking very beautiful, straightening her skirt while she engages in a conversation with the young guy. Roscoe and Gaylin had taken their seats, while their dates prepared to go up to the buffet to get their dinner. A waitress walks over to the table and Gaylin is caught off guard, still staring at Chloe who is now sauntering to a table with the guy holding her hand.

"What y'all folks gon' have to drank?" A deep southern speaking native Tennessee waitress said.

"Oh, just give me a pitcher of beer, that will do me just fine," Roscoe chuckles, laughing aloud.

"You sho' is funny. You sho' you don't want nuthin'else, like tea?" The deep southern said. "Us ain't got no beer."

"Just bring us a large pitcher of lemonade, ma'am," Roscoe said, smiling at Carla who is walking towards the table with a plate of food in her hand.

Gaylin is still lustfully watching Chloe as his date notices his disrespectful demeanor when she takes a seat, holding a small bowl of neatly prepared tossed salad.

"She's not all that. I have more butt and breasts than that fashion doll," CeCe said, rolling her eyes at Gaylin.

"Oh, I wasn't looking at her. I thought that was one of the guys from the office," he lied, trying to hide his expression.

Chloe excuses herself from the young man and goes to the restroom to wash her hands before she eats dinner. Gaylin's eyes follow her as he sips on a glass of lemonade that the waitress recently brought over to the table.

"I'll be back, baby. I'm going to the rest room," he said to CeCe, who is eating her tossed salad covered in Ranch dressing and shredded cheese.

However, when Chloe walks out of the restroom, she runs into Gaylin who is standing outside the ladies' restroom, sneakily glancing around with his hands folded across his chest. He quickly pushes her back into the bathroom and covers her mouth with his hand. A middle-aged white lady attempts to wash her hands at the sink before taking a fearful glimpse at the man who rushes her out of the restroom.

"Get out old lady!" Gaylin shouts, still covering Chloe's mouth who is extremely horror-stricken.

"I'm sorry about today. It will never happen again," He apologetically said, releasing his hand from over her mouth. "You're so beautiful and I couldn't control myself."

"Stay away from me, you creep!" She shouts as a young woman walks into the bathroom. "The only reason your black behind isn't in jail because of your wife! I don't want to see her hurt anymore. I prayed for you and God will punish your sorry butt one day."

Chloe dashes out of the restroom back to the table where her date is sitting. CeCe is glancing in that direction as Gaylin proudly strolls back smiling from ear to ear.

"Are you trying to get in her pants, too?" CeCe sneers. "If so, let me know and I'll leave you two alone."

"No, it's not like that. I don't know that girl." Gaylin smiles at Roscoe and they all continue to eat their meals.

One hour has passed and Dion is still driving downtown on the busy streets in Miami in search for her husband. But when she approaches a four-lane traffic stop, she glimpses over at a nearby restaurant and spots Roscoe's old beat up pickup truck. She angrily makes a U-turn in the middle of oncoming traffic and speeds over to the facility.

Dion parks the car and closes her eyes and imagines Roscoe in that restaurant having a romantic dinner with a beautiful woman. She quickly forces her mind to think positive, but that thought is surely interrupted when she sees Roscoe from the outside window, laughing and having a good time with a young girl that looks half his age. Therefore, she madly opens her car's trunk with her keys and grabs a hand full of Roscoe's clothes and storms into the restaurant where common folks are engaging in sweet conversation. Dion runs hysterically into the place with a hand full of Roscoe's belongings. She pushes a waitress into the salad bar. Bewildered people look around as if a freak show is about to happen.

Dion approaches the table and throws Roscoe's dirty clothes, muddy shoes and other attires on top of their hot meals. Ketchup, honey mustard and country-style ribs find their way onto the girls' nicely groomed outfits; CeCe and Carla are startled.

"I want your sour breath, raggedy-mouth butt out my house!" Dion shouts, and then slaps him in the face with an open hand.

"Baby, wait, I can explain." He gets up from the table and races behind her. She is walking fast almost out of the restaurant.

"I'm sick and tired of you treating me like this!" She slams her fist down on a table where people are eating, drinks spill on their laps.

"Baby, I can explain," Roscoe pleads with tears in his eyes.

"No need to explain!" She throws her hands up in the air while walking off. "Your junk will be sitting out front when you walk outside! And, oh, you can forget seeing this baby. You will never see this child once it's born," She said with a bold voice, rubbing her stomach.

"Sweetheart let me explain. I love you. I made a mistake," Roscoe sorrowfully said with tears flowing down his face.

"Stop crying like a little wimp! You should of thought about our love before you stepped out on our marriage! I don't want you anymore, so I hope that chicken head, ghetto freak heifer can give you a place to stay!" Dion said. She holds back the tears as she feels them stinging in her eyes.

Fifteen:
Death Caught You Sneaking

The long ride home seems quite distant as Dion's Beige Malibu weaves its way into the narrow driveway where Roscoe's old pickup truck is parked in the yard. She instantly feels an urge to scream in anger, but the tears flowing down her face wouldn't allow it. She turns off the ignition, grabs her purse and walks into her dark home where all the lights are turned off.

"Hello, baby." Roscoe meets her at the door with a boutique of roses.

Dion continues to walk past him, ignoring his gestures to be a good man.

"Baby, I know I messed up, but I promise to make it up to you," he said, following her into the kitchen like a sick puppy. He flips on the light and puts down the flowers.

Dion is still silent with tear crust on her face. Roscoe embraces her into his arms and releases a warm kiss on her cheek.

"Baby, I love you. I don't want anybody but you. Sometimes men don't know what they got until it's almost gone. Baby, I messed up and I want to prove to you that I'm a good man."

Dion breaks freely from Roscoe's embrace and stares deeply at the wall in disbelief with her hands folded across her chest.

"Darling, say something. Don't give me the silent treatment. I'm sorry. I'm so sorry for messing up," he said to her while looking at her from behind.

Teardrops fall down her face as she reaches into the cabinet and grabs a black pot and fills it up with cold water.

She sits the pot on the stove and turns the temperature to boiling.

"Baby, say something, please, I said I'm sorry."

The temperature on the pot is rising; steam is surfacing around the stove. Dion goes to the food pantry and pulls out an open box. She grabs the one-third measuring cup and prepares a serving for one person. She adds a teaspoon of salt and pours the one third into the pot and stirs it slowly.

"Baby, what do you want me to do? I said I messed up."

Dion continues to stir slowly and then turns down the stove's temperature to medium-low and covers the pot with a lid. Roscoe is still standing behind her.

"Well, since you don't want to talk, I'm going to bed. This is still my house," he said rudely, strutting away as if he owns the whole world.

Roscoe goes into the bedroom where he and Dion sleep. He takes off all his clothing, except for his faded out, used to be blue boxers. His cell phone vibrates and he answers it.

"Yeah, hello," he speaks into the mouthpiece.

"How did it go?" The voice said.

"Gaylin, man, everything went great. She's not going anywhere. I have her empty head all wrapped around my fingers, and when she comes to bed tonight, I'm knocking some boots. I'm going to tear that thang up."

Roscoe soon disconnects his call and is unaware that Dion has been standing in the doorway listening to the whole conversation. He reaches across the end table and turns on a CD by Gregory Jones,' *I Feel Good Tonight.*' The bedroom is dark, with a glimpse of moonlight shining through the partially closed window blinds. He lays in his king size bed on his back with his hands tucked underneath his head with his eyes close. *I feel good. I feel good tonight.* He mimics Gregory Jones' lyrics to the song that is playing.

Reminiscing in deep thought as the song brings back sweet memories to Roscoe, who could hear Dion's footsteps tip toeing down the hallway. The sudden smell of buttered grits and toast remind him of breakfast in bed when he first met Dion some time ago. *Oh, how I would love breakfast in bed again. Hot buttered grits and ham!* He thinks with a smile.

Racing into the room like a mad woman without a clue, Dion throws a very hot pot of steaming, buttered grits on Roscoe that leaves him running around and shouting in a raging fit. She turns on the light, holding a disposable camera in her hand.

Snap. Snap. She takes a picture of Roscoe as he brushes the soaked grits off his peeled burned skin, bubbling with thick yellowish pus. *Snap. Snap.* Dion takes another picture while he angrily races towards her with pink bloody burned lips.

"You crazy witch! You stupid lunatic!" He attempts to slap her in the face but stops dead in his tracks when she sarcastically starts singing.

Three weeks later, on a bright sunny Sunday morning, Dion prances in the mirror, combing down her nicely wrapped hair with gospel music being heard in the background. She is preparing to attend church worship services and is overjoyed that she had cleaned all of Roscoe's belongings out of the house. He is living downtown in a tacky-looking boarder room, just a few miles from her home. There's gossip talk going around the neighborhood that she came home early one day and scaled Roscoe almost to death with hot water when she found him in her bed with a younger woman. The constant rumors bring a smile upon her face because now she is known as a courageous black woman that is not afraid to confront a cheating mate.

Ring. Ring. The doorbell startles Dion, she turns down her radio and walks to the front door and opens it.

"What do you want?" She said to him in a hostile tone.

"Baby, I still love you. Can I please come back home?" Roscoe said, standing in the doorway looking a hot mess with crusty pink chapped lips.

"Negro, get from my door or else this time it will be bleach I throw on you," she said, attempting to close the door.

"Baby, baby, please, I made a mistake. I made a mistake," He cries aloud, tucking his ashy hands into his urine stained pants pocket.

Dion takes a deep breath and thinks for a brief moment. Her love for Roscoe goes much deeper than what she ever had for anyone. But seeing him in the arms of another woman had brought on much hate and animosity.

"Get your pissy smelling butt from my front door!" I don't have time to play games with you, Roscoe! I'm on my way to church!" She slams the door shut and stands still, staring at it. She could hear him sobbing and mumbling to himself as he walks down from off the porch.

"God forgives us because he loves us! God makes us as clean as freshly fallen snow! We must forgive others! I'm just a stranger in this land passing through with the help of God! God forgives, why can't you?" Roscoe shouts while looking back at the house.

Tears roll down Dion's face as the door flings open. She runs outside and jumps in the arms of Roscoe.

"I forgive you! I forgive you!" She said, holding him tightly.

"Oh, baby. I'm sorry. I'm truly sorry. I want to do right. Let's go to church together."

"But, Roscoe, you look like you've slept the whole week in those clothes. You can't go to church looking like that," she said, observing his filthy appearance.

"I don't care, baby. God says to come as you are. I'm going to church with you and don't care what nobody says."

Dion rocks with the beat as she moves along with the choir who is singing a soulful gospel song. Roscoe sits beside her and observes some of the members whispering and sneering in their direction. Reverend Bowie is already on his tired feet from preaching a week's long revival at a church seventy miles away. He makes his way to the pulpit as the congregation stands like they do in the courtroom when the judge appears.

"Glory be to the Father. Praise His Holy name." Reverend Bowie's deep voice filled around the Holy Spirit filled room.

"God is so good. Let us give him all the praises for allowing us to see another new day." He patted the perspiration from his face. "If it wasn't for His grace and mercy, some of us would be dead."

"Amen," the congregation said in unison.

"Let us bow our heads in prayer and give God the glory because He is our source and protector."

"Glory, halleluiah!" A woman said who is raising her hands to the Heavens.

"Lord, help us to be faithful to your word and to not allow the enemy to corrupt our minds with ungodly things." His eyes close. "Guide our footsteps and embed a clean and loving heart."

"Amen," the congregation said in unison.

"Lord, I thank you for the many blessings you have bestowed upon my life and continue to allow my faithfulness to bring more soldiers to your army because this is a winning battle."

"Halleluiah, thank you, Jesus!" A woman shouts, shaking her head with tears rolling down her face.

"Lord, you're a doctor who has never lost a patient, and a lawyer who has never lost a case. I thank you, Father, Oh, I thank you." His eyes still close and hands stretched out.

Roscoe peeps over at Dion with his eyes partially open.

"There's no greater gift than the love of God. Lord helps us to love thy neighbors as thyself. Give us the strength to move everyday so that we can be a witness for your Word."

"Amen," the congregation said in unison.

"Lord, save all souls and let everyone know that he/ she can't get to Heaven without first repentance of sins, acknowledge who you are, and be spirit filled with the Holy Ghost."

"Praise God's Holy name. Praise Him!" An elderly lady stands up and shouts, waving her hands from side to side.

"I don't care about how much money you got in the bank, or how big your house is. If you're not ready when your time comes, then Hell you shall see. I don't care about your platinum credit Visa Card. There's no such thing as a payment plan to Heaven. Either you got it, or you don't. No postponements or delays."

"Amen," everyone said in unison while clapping hands.

Dion and Roscoe are doing much better since he gave his life to Christ two months ago. The lustful thoughts of other women and the late night outings have long freed his mind. He is more committed to God who has given him another chance at life. Dion's enormous belly is rapidly growing with the baby twisting and turning in every direction. She sleeps peacefully on her man's lap while he reads the Bible. His anointed mood is interrupted with a loud knock coming from the front door. He eases his wife's head out of his lap, and places the Bible on the sofa and goes to open the door.

"What's up, dawg? No time, no see. Where you been hiding?" Gaylin happily said, standing in the doorway with a six-pack of beer.

"Nothing much, man. I'm sort of busy. You mind coming back later," Roscoe dryly said.

"Busy? That's what you been saying for two months now. What's going on?" He said with attitude.

"Man, I said I'm busy. I don't have time to talk." Roscoe speaks softly, trying not to awake Dion.

"Oh, it's that witch wife of yours, right? After she almost killed your crazy butt you still want to be with her. Man you crazy," Gaylin chuckles, peeping over Roscoe's shoulders into the house. "Where is that witch anyway?"

Roscoe takes a deep breath and anger grows in his heart.

"Where is that stiff, big pregnant witch? I know she's the reason you acting like a strung out sex whipped punk." He chuckles again, attempting to walk in the house.

"Hold up, player. Where do you think you're going?" Roscoe blocks his path with his two hundred pound body frame.

"Inside. The fights are on and you know we use to watch it on television every Friday night," he said, pushing Roscoe aside and walks boldly into the house.

Gaylin walks into the house and sees Dion lying on the sofa with slob coming from her mouth. Roscoe is angry, but keep silent for a brief moment.

"Oh, here's the witch. Right here lying on the sofa with her big beer belly," Gaylin laughs as he walks near her.

Dion sluggishly yawns and awakes from her sleep and then notices that Gaylin is in the house. She quickly regains composure as if she is the Energizer Bunny.

"What are you doing in my house? You're not welcomed here anymore!" She shouts, as she jumps up like ravaging wolves.

"I'm here to watch the fights. You know me and Roscoe use to watch the fights together every Friday night," he said.

"Not tonight, right Roscoe?" Dion said to Roscoe who is standing around the corner afraid to speak his mind.

"Roscoe, stop acting like a wimp, you need to put this woman in her place and let her know who wears the pants in this house. She got you acting all sweet, like a faggot," Gaylin said, as he plops down on the sofa and open a can of beer.

"Look, sucker! You got one second to get the heck out of my house or the grave you shall see!" Dion yells, shaking a finger at him.

"Okay. I'll go." He stands up with the beer in his hand and walks towards the door. "But, Roscoe, man, you've changed. Just wait until the boys at the pool hall finds out about you. You got more sugar in your tank than I thought." Roscoe looks away in disbelief while those hurtful degrading words pieced his soul.

For the past few months, Dion sensed an evil force manifesting inside of Roscoe that sends cold chills flowing down her spine. Unknown phone calls have been coming through rapidly, and he has not read the Bible or attended church services since he began hanging out in the street with strange people who appear as if they've been rejected by society. She knows that this is not good, so she takes everything to God in prayer.

She later learns that her husband had backslid from the word of God. He was a heavy heroin addict that abused illegal drugs and used most of their lifetime savings to fulfill his addiction. However, early one morning around two o'clock, Dion hears a knock on the front door from two police officers stating that she had to come down to the morgue and identify her husband's nude body that they found in a vacant, dilapidated, drug infested house along with an unidentified prostitute.

Part 3

Nowhere to Hide

Sixteen:
Hot as Hell

Dion's small-framed cozy home is filled with people comforting her about the loss of Roscoe. Her eyes beam in anger as she glares at Roscoe's sister who is carelessly packing all of his unkempt belongings in a brown paper bag. Saddie, Nadine and Gail gaze around in disbelief at Roscoe's inconsiderate relatives, who apparently forgot that Dion is still his wife. Dion madly pushes her chair from the table.

"Wait one cotton picking minute! I want all you fools to put my husband's junk back right where you found them!" She shouts, spit flying from her mouth. "You all can take your crazy butts back to Georgia!"

Roscoe's sister stops dead in her tracks, flashing a sly grin with her bony hands on her hips.

"We're not leaving until after my brother's funeral." Her voice had a bitter edge.

"Oh yeah. Well, you all better get to stepping, because the funeral is over," Dion said, marching to the front door and opening it. Roscoe's sixty-year-old mother jumps up from her chair like an acrobat performing in a circus.

"What? What do you mean over? He just died!" Roscoe's mother growls, blasting a stale scent of mothballs.

"Like I said, the funeral is over. So you fools can get to stepping," Dion said, still holding the door open with madness settling in her spirit.

Saddie, Nadine and Gail are galvanized. They glare around at Dion without saying a word.

"Where's my boy's body? We're taking him on back to Cherry Hill. Right where all his people are buried," The mother said while walking up to her, swaying back and forth with attitude.

"Roscoe isn't going to be buried nowhere! I'm burning his sorry behind up!" She snaps harshly like a bitter woman.

"You're what?" Roscoe's family shouts in unison.

"I'm burning the no good sucker up! He's not having a funeral!" She said, hands pressed down on her hips, ready for a fight.

"You can't do that! I won't allow you to burn up my child! What kind of wife are you?" The mother said. Her voice trembles as she takes a seat in the armchair.

Gail and Nadine make eye contact with one another before speaking.

"Dion, I think you should think about it before you have Roscoe's body cremated," Gail said, as she sits in her wheelchair. "This is his family, too. This is their final chance to say their last goodbyes."

"I don't give a hoot! Roscoe doesn't deserve to have a funeral! Funerals are for dignified folks who have left a legacy behind, someone who has contributed to society and has something to be remembered for! All Roscoe left behind was a bunch of bills and me an STD!" She shouts, slamming the door shut as she races to the kitchen table.

Saddie and Nadine run behind her, leaving Roscoe's relatives in the living room, mumbling words among themselves.

"An STD? Oh, Dion I'm so sorry," Nadine said, giving her a sisterly hug with a touch of sadness glowing on her face.

"Child, I'll burn that no good dog up, too," Saddie said. "He gave you an STD?"

"Heck yeah! That low down dirty Roscoe slept around with some crabby hoochie and brought the mess home to me! I just found out when I went to the doctor for my monthly checkup! My baby better not come out looking half crazy and retarded!" She said eyes red with rage.

"Just pray about it. Everything will be okay," Nadine said softly.

"I hate Roscoe! That's why I'm burning his butt up!" She shouted voice loud enough for his family to hear in the other room.

"Dion, I don't think that's the right way to handle it. Think about his family. They don't deserve to be punished for Roscoe's wrong doings. Just give him a proper burial and let God handle the rest. God knows what to do," Nadine said with care.

"I don't care! I'm burning Roscoe's behind up! I'm giving him an early preview of hell!" Dion said, her voice very cold and distant. "He done me wrong and I have no sympathy for him."

"That's the way! Teach that scum bag a lesson. Let him know that even in death his butt will still pay the price!" Saddie chuckles, glancing back towards the living room where Roscoe's relatives are preparing to leave the house.

"This is not a laughing matter. Dion, please, think about what you're doing. You still love Roscoe and what will you tell the baby when he or she grows up. Are you going to tell him or her that you cremated their father because you had a chip on your shoulder?" Nadine said too soft-spoken.

"Heck yeah. I'm going to tell my child that I burned her no good daddy up and then I flushed his ashes right down the toilet along with my doo-doo," Dion said with much pride, smiling back at Saddie.

Roscoe's bony leg sister peers her angry face into the kitchen where Dion, Saddie, and Nadine were having a personal conversation about Roscoe's final remains.

"We're going to get my brother's body and there's not a darn thing you can do about it!"

"Oh, yeah, if you didn't know, Roscoe was still my husband and I'm the only one that has the first and last word to say about where I want him to be buried. So I advise you all to get to stepping before all hell break loose right in this house."

Constant gossip escalated around the community that Dion cremated Roscoe's body out of hate and animosity. They heard she had felt that after he backslid from the word of God and began to pick up on his old evil habits that it claimed his life before his first child was born.

In another sense, Roscoe's death affected Gaylin a great deal. He secluded himself from family and friends and spent many late evenings exercising at the gym. But one night after a long strenuous, tiresome workout, he doses off in a deep sleep while relaxing on a bench near the dressing room.

"Death will soon come for you," the voice said. Gaylin wiggles and cringes in his sleep.

"Death waits for no one. Are you ready?" The soft speaking voice said.

Gaylin twists and turns and tries to awake from his deep sleep, but his eyes are glued shut, unable to open.

"Where will you spend eternity? Your soul is on its way to hell. Your soul will be tossed into the lake of fire that burns with sulfur and brimstone, joining the beast and all wickedness. You shall be tormented day and night forever and endless moment."

Gaylin's heart is racing fast as he tries to move his body that is frozen stiff, lying flat on his back, like a dead man in a casket. *Who knowing the judgment of God, that they which commit such things, are worthy of death, not only do the same, but have pleasure in them that do them. Hell is a place of weeping and God will punish those who do not turn from their sin.*

White angels as pure as snow; stand sadly around Gaylin's coffin as a headless beast douses kerosene in a can, pouring a heavy trail around him. The beast laughs and strikes a match and throws it on the coffin. The fire rages and rushes into the casket, burning up Gaylin's stiff body. He feels the agonizing pain, but is unable to move. He tries to pray silently and a voice utters, *"It's too late your time has come."* The flames sweeps across him again, scrapes his flesh to the naked bone. The stench of his burning flesh consumes the room that has engulfed in flames.

"Sir, are you okay? Sir, are you okay?!" A white security officer said, while shaking Gaylin uncontrollably who is yelling in a frenzy manner.

Gaylin's eyes pop wide open; he is drenched in sweat from head to toe.

"Where am I?" He asked, confusedly glancing around the gym.

"Sir, you're at Mike's Gold Gym. Remember? You have a membership here," the security officer said.

"Oh, yeah." He remembered, still perplexed and confound.

"Sir, would you like for me to call someone to take you home? You're not acting just right," The officer said, looking down at Gaylin who is shivering, afraid of his own shadow.

"No, No, I'm alright. I just had a bad dream. I'll be going now," he said before stumbling over and falling to the floor.

"Sir, stay here. I'll call an ambulance. You don't have any business driving home." The man attempts to call for help on his cell phone.

"No! I said I'm okay! I don't need an ambulance!" Gaylin snapped back, trying to control his weak balance.

Gaylin staggers to his car, drenched in sweat as he thinks of his frightening dream that left a puzzled look in his eyes. He slowly pulls out his keys from inside his gym shorts and opens his door. He gets inside the car and blankly stares away into the night air. When he arrives home, Mrs.

Bradford is putting Gail into the bed, while Jamal crawls on the floor babbling out baby words.

"Hey, honey, you're home. I hope you're not mad about Mama coming over to help me. We figured that you probably would be tied up at the office tonight," Gail said, flashing a glorious smile at him as he walks pass the bedroom, still in a daze.

"Gaylin, are you okay?" Mrs. Bradford said before pacing to the bedroom's entrance where she sees him sitting on the floor curled up in a ball like a scared child.

He glares up at her with tear struck eyes as he shouts hysterically in a raging fit.

"I don't want to die and go to hell! I don't want to go to hell!"

Seventeen:
Brown-Eyed Devil

Cooked turkey with all the trimmings was set before Gaylin, Gail and Lyndia on this Thanksgiving Day of 2002. It was freezing cold outside, sort of odd for Florida's normal warm temperature. Monice rushes into the unlocked house, wearing a thick, heavy black leather coat with matching boots. Inside the home now reeks with her strong-scented fragrance that lingers around like an air freshener. Mrs. Bradford soon brings to the table a pot full of collard greens and ham hocks.

"It's cold outside," Monice said, while shivering as she takes off her thick black coat and places it on the sofa. "Something smells good in here."

"We're in the dining room," Mrs. Bradford said, uncovering plastic wrap from off a chocolate-coated pecan pie.

"Yummy." Monice glances at the food on the table. "I'm going to gain an extra ten pounds after this holiday season."

"Child, a little meat on them bones isn't going to hurt nothing." Mrs. Bradford stated, unwrapping a sweet potato pie.

Gail wheels herself closer to the table, as Gaylin grabs her hand in happiness, before saying the grace over the meal that the Lord has blessed. Jamal is sitting in his highchair, tosses crumbled chips on the floor. Gaylin had given himself to God and has promised to be a better man. They both attend the same church and always read the Bible together as a family.

"Let us bow our heads and give God thanks for this good food that I stayed up all night and prepared," Mrs. Bradford said as she seats down in a chair next to Lyndia.

"Heavenly Father, thank you for allowing us to see another Thanksgiving Day, blesses this food before us and blesses the hands that prepared it. Heavenly Father, we give you all the praises and glory Amen," Gaylin said as he opens his eyes with a pleasant smile. The family feasts and enjoys their holiday dinner, exchanging pleasant conversation while the cold winter wind blows hard on the rooftop.

Later that night when all the family had gone their separate ways, Gaylin prepared to put Gail to bed, but was interrupted with the vibration of his cell phone moving around in his pocket. He quickly retrieves it, not knowing who is on the other end.

"I haven't heard from you in months. Why haven't you called?" The lady asked, smacking on gum in the earpiece.

Gaylin holds his phone as he looks at the Bible with Gail staring directly at him.

"Who is it, baby?" Gail asked.

"Nothing to worry about, I'll take this in the next room." He quickly takes the cell phone into the bathroom and briskly closes the door.

"I thought I told you not to call me again." He speaks quietly.

"What? You got a new baby, now. You're not getting rid of me that easily." The lady speaks into the mouthpiece.

"What do you want from me? What the heck do you want?" He angrily said, still trying to talk quietly.

"I want you to leave that crippled witch of yours and come to me and be a real father to your child. You've been playing nurse long enough. It's time to put her butt in a nursing home."

"Listen, woman. That's my wife you're talking about. Do me a favor and don't call me again. Got it?" He disconnects the call and goes back to his bedroom, where Gail is still sitting in her wheelchair with Jamal, lying peacefully in his crib next to their bed.

A few days later after the Thanksgiving holiday had come to a happy ending, Gaylin reported back to work, full of spirit and humming a melody tune to a gospel song that he had heard on the radio before coming to work. He struts in the building carrying his black briefcase and makes his way down the hallway to his office and notices several guys standing around in a corner, admiring a young, blonde-haired woman with full lips and a round face sitting at a desk right across from his.

"Wow, she's fine!" One of the men said while smiling at the woman.

Gaylin strolls into his work cubicle and unloads his briefcase full of important business documents. While he is preparing to begin his workday, a brown-eyed man taps on the window with a sly grin that brings chills down Gaylin's spine.

"Did you see the new hottie? Man, she's something else. That white girl got more booty than two black chicks put together," The man states, smiling from ear to ear.

Gaylin takes a seat in his rocking chair and proceeds to make his daily business calls without commenting on what the man had previously said.

"Man, did you hear me?" He speaks louder and walks closer. "I said have you checked out the new office girl? She's the bomb! I know you want to hit that."

"Hello, Mr. Simpson, this is Gaylin Harris," Gaylin said to the client on the telephone, still ignoring the brown-eyed man, who is now invading his personal space.

"So, it's like that, now. You're trying to ignore me," the man said to Gaylin, who is still talking on the telephone. The guy then rudely disconnects the call by unplugging the telephone right in the middle of an important conversation.

"Hello, Mr. Simpson. Mr. Simpson?" Gaylin said while tapping on the phone's receiver, trying to reconnect the call.

"I unplugged the darn phone," the man said, holding the cord in his hand.

"Why did you do a stupid thing like that? I was in the middle of making a deal, you idiot!" Gaylin shouted.

"I'm sorry, man, but I had to get your attention somehow or another."

"What do you want, Dexter? I have a million things that I need to get done today," Gaylin said, with very firm expression.

"Did you see the new girl? Man, she's sweet, body so tight and fine."

"Is that what this is all about? Dexter, I don't have time for nonsense. I have a lot of work to do. So will you please take the gossip somewhere else, because I'm very busy." His face expressed an agitated expression.

"What? You're passing down a perfect opportunity to get in the panties? Man, I don't believe it. What did your wife feed you over the holidays?" Dexter said with a crooked smile.

"Dexter, will you please leave? I'm quite busy and don't have time to talk," Gaylin said, as he fumbles through papers that are scattered over his desk.

While they continue to talk, the new blonde-haired woman peers her pretty round face into Gaylin's cubicle holding a stack of folders.

"Excuse me, which one of you are Gaylin Harris?" She said softly.

"He is!" Dexter shouts in excitement, as he points to Gaylin, who is staring deeply at the nice curvy-framed woman.

"Mr. Simpson on line two left you a message saying that he is ready to close on that Parkinson's deal. I pulled out the files for you. All you have to do now is just sign the documents after the attorney looks over everything," She said while giving her blonde hair a toss.

"Ah, Man! How about that!" Gaylin said as he leaps from his desk in happiness. Thank you so much, ma'am!"

"Oh, you're quite welcome." She places the folders on his desk and adjusts her tight-fitted skirt and scoots out of the office room.

"Man, did you see that butt? Did you see that nice big butt?" Dexter said in lust as Gaylin still smiles trying to consume all of the good news.

"Let's go and celebrate. You deserve to be treated like a king after you got Mr. Simpson to close on that deal. We're looking at a whopping six-figure income."

"Yeah. Let's hit the road. I can afford to take a three hour lunch break today," Gaylin said, while placing the stack of folders into his locked cabinet.

"What about her?" Dexter said, pointing a finger at the nicely built new worker. "I'm not going if she isn't."

"What about her?"

"Aren't you going to invite her along? She did take the call for you after I unplugged it. She deserves some reward."

"I've already thanked her. No need to go overboard with it. I'm going on home to tell my lovely wife about our new beginning," Gaylin said, as he places a few papers into his black briefcase.

"Man, are you nuts? There's a sexy, fine woman all up in your face who wants to give you the panties and you would rather pass that up? You must be some kind of fool," he said boldly, flashing a frown.

"Dexter, have you forgotten that I'm a married man?"

"Ha. Ha. Married? That's never stopped you."

"Well, something happened a few months ago that changed my life. I'm now a born-again Christian who lives for the Lord," Gaylin said with much pride as he attempts to walk out of the office.

"Are you serious? Man, stop all this bull saying you a born-again Christian. You're no Christian than the man on the moon," Dexter chuckles, as the other guys look on.

"I don't have to explain anything to you fools. I'm outta here," Gaylin said as he storms out the office.

"Wait, man!" I'm sorry!" Dexter said.

Gaylin stops in his tracks and glances back at him.

"I'm sorry, player." Dexter gives him a brotherly hug. "Are you still coming to my bachelor's party on Christmas Eve?"

"I don't know about that. I think I might stay at home with my family," Gaylin unsurely said.

"Man, come on. It's my last night of freedom. You said you all saved and is a born-again Christian. Maybe you can come over and help bring some of us to Jesus," Dexter said as his brown eyes narrow.

Gaylin grins broadly; his face lit up like a Christmas tree.

"Alright. I'll be more honored to come to your bachelor's party. God needs more good soldiers in His army and my presence would surely do the trick."

Gaylin struts away while humming a gospel song and smiling gloriously. Dexter slyly eases over quietly to the next cubicle where a guy is working diligently at his desk.

"Hey, Charlie, I want you to get started on finding the hottest, sexist women in this city to perform at my bachelor's party on Christmas Eve." *This will be one Christmas Gaylin will never forget,* Dexter thinks with his evil brown eyes staring off, as they stretch wide open.

Eighteen:
Backdoor Santa

Christmas Eve arrived very swiftly, with people out and about in shopping malls trying to gather their last minute Christmas presents. Gail and her friends, Dion, Saddie and Nadine are all happily at a church Christmas party for the children. Gaylin is decked out, in a two-piece matching outfit with a thick gold chain around his neck, preparing to attend his co-worker's bachelor's party that will be held at the home of one of the fraternity brothers.

Gaylin jumps in his sporty black Corvette, sticks the key in the ignition and drives off to the exotic celebration in high speed. Upon arrival, the beautiful two-story brick home in a predominantly white neighborhood wasn't hard to find with the loud hip hop music being played, and the long line of exotic cars with men standing around, smoking blunts and drinking beer out of plastic cups.

He can hear people laughing and cheering like they're having a great time as he parks his ride in the driveway of a vacant house next door. He walks pass a few rowdy men cursing and drinking alcohol straight from the bottle. Dexter meets him at the front door with a wide grin on his face and the smell of stale sex and smoke sends Gaylin into a coughing fit.

"What's up, Dawg? I see you made it," Dexter said, escorting Gaylin into the smoke filled house where a few couples are stretched out on the couch, kissing like no one is around. There were ladies in skimpy, fitted skirts with colored hair, sitting near them, like they're waiting for their turn.

"Dude, what's going on in here? It smells like you all been smoking weed and screwing each other all day," He said in between coughs, fanning his way in through the smoke.

"Man, we have been partying since this morning. Them stuck up behind neighbors already sent the police over here four times, saying that we're disturbing the peace. Heck, I told the cops that today is my last day of freedom, and I'm going to enjoy it," Dexter said, handing Gaylin a plastic cup of champagne.

"No, partner, I don't drink anymore," He said, turning away from the cup.

"Oh, my bad, I forgot that you're a born-again Christian." *We'll see after tonight,* Dexter thought.

"I thought this supposed to be a bachelor party. What are women doing here? It seems more like an unrestrained orgy," Gaylin said, glancing around the room.

"Dawg, take it easy. Sit back and enjoy yourself. This is a different kind of bachelor's party. The kind that will go down in player's history," Dexter chuckles, sipping on champagne in a glass.

"I'm only here for a few minutes. I promised my wife that I'll be home early to enjoy Christmas Eve with her and the baby."

"Hey, Dawg, you can leave whenever. I'm just honored that you're here," Dexter said with a sly grin. "Let me get everyone inside because the party is about to get started."

Gaylin then makes himself comfortable as if he's at home, by lying back on the couch and placing his legs on the coffee table, humming a gospel song. But that is soon interrupted with Dexter hollering and announcing that a sexy, most gorgeous backdoor Santa has arrived. The DJ immediately pops in a CD that has vulgar degrading lyrics.

A beautiful, nutmeg brown skin girl, with hair so beautiful, strolls into the room wearing red and white exotic silky thongs and a very short red and white Santa Clause jacket, exposing her breasts and the tattoo on her butt. She struts around in her three-inch heel stilettos as men shout in lust, while the CD plays in the background.

"Ooh, shake it, baby!" A man shouts from the living room.

Gaylin takes a glimpse of the dancer and lets out a gust of air. He fumbles in his pockets for his keys and makes a fast exit to the front door. Dexter takes another sip of champagne and walks over to the stripper who is parading herself around like a paid hooker, and whispers in her ear. She nods in agreement with a crooked smile, and her eyes beckon another dancer to take over, while she races outside behind Gaylin.

Gaylin angrily jumps in his car and attempts to start the engine, but the beautiful Backdoor Santa, captures his attention when he looks at her gorgeous face, while she bangs on his car window.

"Sir, are you coming back inside," she said, staring back at the house.

"CeCe?" Gaylin said, staring at her as he rolls down the window.

"Oh my God, Gaylin!" She said, covering her mouth in shock. "What are you doing here?"

"No, the question is, what are you doing here?" He asked.

"This is my side gig. I do this to help pay my way through school."

"Girl, you have no business working as a stripper. Why are you doing this? The fast food joints don't pay enough anymore?" He said, sounding like a concern parent.

"I had to get a real job when your butt stopped supporting me," she said with attitude. "Remember, you paid my tuition and all of my car payments?"

Gaylin sits silently in his car for a brief moment and notices a barrage of flashing lights and police sirens coming down the street.

"CeCe, get in, quick! The cops are coming here to raid this place!" He shouts and cranks his engine.

The girl jumps in the car and he speeds away quickly as he sees the officers from his review mirror kicking Dexter's door down and running in the house like mad dogs. He drives down the street, bouncing his head in happiness to his gospel song and CeCe then places her hand on his thighs and moves it slowly between his legs. He pushes her hands away.

"CeCe, I'm a changed man now. I thought you understood that when I broke it off with you," He said with an irritated look.

"Yeah. That's what they all say. But I don't buy it with you. You're different."

 She leans over and kisses him on the cheek and takes off her Santa jacket, exposing her breast.

"Girl, stop it, now!" He swerves across the street. "I'm a changed man! I don't fool around like that anymore!"

CeCe pulls off her cherry scented thong underwear and throws them in his face.

"Smell it! You know you want some of this sweet juice!"

Gaylin pulls over on the side of the busy street and angrily gets out of the car and yanks CeCe's naked body out from the passenger's side.

"Get to stepping, freak!" He shouts, people staring from their cars in shock.

"Oh, it's like that now!" She said, while covering her nakedness. "You can't do me like this!"

"Oh, yeah, watch me!" Gaylin races back to his car and attempts to drive away.

"You're not getting away with this! I'm going to scream rape and your sorry behind is going to jail!" She shouts. "You're not going to screw me and get away with it!"

Gaylin turns on the ignition and shouts back to her from the window.

"I never had intentions on leaving my wife! You were just a quick fix until I made my way to the next whore! You don't even know me!" He shouts, as he throws her clothes to her and speeds off.

"I'll get you, you creep!" She shouts back.

Gaylin later arrives home, tired and sleepy after taking a long drive to Hollywood, Florida just to clear his mind of all the hidden secrets that are terrorizing his life. He walks into the dark house and finds Gail fast asleep, sitting up in her wheelchair with the baby on her lap. He kisses her on the cheek and whispers in her ear that he is home. She then awakes, with drool coming down from her mouth.

"You're home early. How was the bachelor's party?" She said in between a yawn.

"It got a little crazy, so I decided to leave. You know how wild those things can get," he said as he takes Jamal off her lap and places him in his crib.

When Gaylin prepares to get himself and Gail ready for bed, he hears a loud noise coming from outside, like a window shattering. His alarm system in his sporty Corvette, that's parked in the driveway, starts to sound loudly.

"What's that honey?" Gail said with concern, eyes glancing around the room. Gaylin then places her in bed and reaches inside the drawer and pulls out his Glock and runs out of the bedroom.

He runs angrily out of the house in his boxers and wife beater t-shirt and notices that the tinted windows to his sporty car are broken. He marches over closer to the vehicle and sees a DVD lying on the seat with broken glass scattered everywhere. The DVD is labeled in bright bold letters: *Got You Sucker! By CeCe the tattoo stripper*.

He immediately grabs the DVD from off the seat and throws it to the ground, stomping on it with his foot. While he is stomping and destroying the video item, a black tinted window Cadillac, stops near his house and a voice utters, "There's more where that came from, partner." The car drives off in high speed.

Nineteen:
Heartache Hotel

After the Christmas holiday and only a few days left before another new year, Gaylin sits nervously while tapping his fingers on his work desk. His telephone is ringing constantly, and he blankly stares at it as if it's invisible.

"Dawg, are you going to get that?" Dexter asked, looking straight at the ringing phone from the entrance.

"Partner, don't call me 'dawg' anymore. The name is Gaylin," he said with an attitude.

"My bad. You didn't seem to care when you were screwing half of Miami," Dexter sarcastically said while walking off.

"What did you say, partner?" Gaylin asked furiously, walking behind him with a balled fist. "Man, I'm not in the mood to play games this morning."

"I said_"

Gaylin cuts him off by sucker punching him in the face with a balled hand. Dexter falls backward onto the coffee machine and nosy co- workers race over to see what is going on.

"That little plan you tried to throw at the bachelor's party didn't work, Dawg," Gaylin said, looking at Dexter who is trying to compose himself from off the floor with spilled coffee stains on his white shirt.

"Hey, I'm just being me. You need to look deep down at yourself and find out who you are, because it sure enough isn't no Christian," Dexter said as he stumbles back to his work station with co- workers looking around in disbelief.

Gaylin walks back to his cubicle and the cute new worker hand delivers a video DVD addressed to him that was left inside the lobby, with bold words printed in red and black: *Got You Sucker! By CeCe, the tattoo stripper.*

"Ah, thank you, ma'am," He said with a forced smile as he takes the DVD. "Someone is always trying to play some kind of joke."

"It doesn't look like a joke to me, sir. It looks more like a bitter woman trying to get even," she said with a sly grin as she strolls off.

Gaylin immediately throws the DVD into his briefcase and grabs his cell phone and angrily goes outside where no one is around. He flips open the phone and dials a number.

"Look, witch! I don't appreciate you trying to ruin my life! If you keep snooping around with your little videotapes, I'm going to kill you! Is that understood?" He snapped into the phone, biting down on his lips.

"What? Who you threatening?" He snaps again into the phone. "Woman I'll beat your brains out! Stay away from me or you'll be sorry!" He disconnects his call and walks back into his office as if nothing is wrong.

Within the next thirty minutes, Gaylin hears his name being called over the intercom system that he has a visitor named CeCe waiting on him in the lobby. Dexter looks at him with a crooked smile and continues to arrange the unorganized papers on his desk. Gaylin adjusts his tie and places a fake smile on his face as the temperature in his body rises in anger at a high degree. He eases out of his chair and walks calmly to the lobby where CeCe is standing around wearing a skimpy tight-fitted black skirt with a red blouse. She holds a video in her hand.

"Hey, honey. Would you like to go out for lunch? I'll pay today," She deviously said, tapping on the DVD.

The secretary in the lobby is being very attentive without constant stares.

"Ah, not today, I'm busy." He attempts to walk away.

"But, Gaylin, I have you DVD." She waves it to him. "I thought you would be eager to see how it all turned out. You know you love to make good videos."

The secretary takes a quick glimpse at the DVD that CeCe is waving around in the air.

"Call me later and I'll see. I have a ton of work to get done before my shift ends," he said, eyes beam with anger as he walks away.

While sitting in his cubicle with a million things running through his mind, he thinks about the sexual video that he made with CeCe, right in his very own home, while his crippled wife lay next door. He knows that if Gail sees the video, she will be devastated enough to end the marriage, taking everything that he struggled hard to pay for. CeCe doesn't have anything to lose, so she cares less about his marriage and his future. *I got to stop her.* He thinks before leaving her a sweet message on her voice mail.

Gaylin meets CeCe at an upscale hotel, not far from where he works. He drives his black Corvette into a vacant parking spot, and watches the young woman get out of her friend's Toyota Camry, carrying an overnight white bag. They greet one another with a hug and walk together, hand-in-hand to the front desk.

"Hello, sir, how can I help you?" The clerk stated, smiling with coffee-stained teeth.

"Yes, I would like a room for tonight," Gaylin said, while fumbling through his wallet for a credit card.

"The room is one hundred and twenty-five dollars per night. You get a continental breakfast delivered to your room and have free access to the pool," The clerk said as Gaylin hands him the credit card.

The man looks down at the card and immediately gives it back to Gaylin.

"I'm sorry sir, but we don't accept those kind of cards. We only accept Master Card, Discover and Visa."

Gaylin retrieves the card and places it back into his wallet. He finds Gail's platinum Visa card tucked away in his wallet, so he decides to use it.

"Here's one. It should be good as new," Gaylin simpers as he hands the clerk the Visa card.

After he pays for the room, they both cheerfully go inside and then CeCe goes into the bathroom to freshen up with a hot steaming shower. Gaylin walks onto the balcony for a breath of fresh air. While he is standing up with his hands tucked deep into his pockets, facing the beautiful end-of-the-year atmosphere, he thinks about his broken promise to God, promising to be a better man. CeCe interrupts that thought when she surprisingly walks up behind him and rubs her nude body against his back

"Come into the shower with me. I have the bathroom all steamed up ready for us," CeCe whispered, caressing him on the back of his neck.

"Not, now. I'll come a little later," he said, while appearing gloomy and sad, staring off in the midnight.

"What's wrong, baby? You act as if you don't want to be here. Wasn't it your idea for us to meet here tonight?" She questioned with a puzzled look.

"I'm sorry. But I have a lot of stuff on my mind," he said, still gazing off like a sick puppy.

"I didn't come here tonight to watch you soil in your own misery," CeCe stated. "I came here to have fun." She embraces him with a tight hug.

Gaylin pushes her against the brick wall and yells, "Would you lay off me! I can't deal with this now!"

CeCe rolls her eyes in madness and runs hysterically into the bathroom. She gets dressed, snatches her overnight bag and attempts to open the door.

"I'm leaving! You can stay your tired butt here! I can do bad all by myself!"

Gaylin stomps in her direction, grabs her belongings out of her hand, and tosses them onto the floor.

"You're not going anywhere," he said, while unbuttoning her blouse and kissing her breast. "I want you. I want you right now."

They aggressively rip off one another clothing and maneuver their way into the strawberry-scented bedroom and make passionate love, as if they are on their honeymoon.

Several hours later, they lay nude in bed drench in sweat and body odor, staring deeply into each other's brown eyes while Gaylin's cell phone vibrates uncontrollably.

"Who is it, honey? That phone has been buzzing since the minute we got here," CeCe asked with irritation.

"It's my wife. She's worried sick about me. Normally, I would have been home to put her to bed. But tonight, she will have to sleep in that wheelchair, because I'm not leaving you here," Gaylin said as he places another sensuous kiss on her lips.

CeCe thinks for a brief moment and embarrassingly pulls away from Gaylin and covers her nakedness with the bed sheets.

"Go home and put your wife to bed. It's bad enough that you're cheating on her. I made a mistake to come here tonight." She jumps out of the bed and fumbles around the room for her clothes. "If I knew that you were a married man from the beginning, I wouldn't have wasted my time. My father is a preacher and this is truly a sin."

"So you're trying to act all self-righteous, now! Don't try to lay the guilt trip on me! You knew that I was married the moment I brought your skank butt to my house!"

"I made a mistake. I'm leaving," she said as she puts on her clothes. "Your wife doesn't deserve to be treated like this."

"You weren't thinking about my dear wife a few hours ago when your freaky behind was all up riding this big horse!" Gaylin shouted, as he furiously gets off the bed.

"Well, I'm entitled to make mistakes in this world. I see now that this is not the life style that I want to live. I want a man who can love me for me, not someone who's just looking for a quick thrill. Go on home to your wife," she said.

"Just wait one minute! Who you think you're talking, too? If it wasn't for me, your broke down family would still be leaving in the ghetto! I'm the one who put them in that upscale neighborhood! I'm the one that helped your cock-eyed daddy get that church loan!" He yelled, while putting on his pants.

"You didn't have anything to do with that! My uncle Ben co- signed for my father to get that church! You're full of bull crap!" CeCe hot headily shouted, as she grabs her belongings, slams the door, and marches to the elevator.

Gaylin is half dressed, exposing his hairy chest; he angrily races behind her where he observes a young couple standing near the elevator.

"Your daddy and your broke down uncle's credit were all screwed up! They didn't have a decent income and thought that their lousy twelve-thousand dollars a year income could purchase them a new church! Man, they must was high on something that day! People from the hood and projects are always looking for a hand out!"

She whirled around and looked him straight in the face. "What do you mean people from the hood and projects are always looking for a hand out? I don't think you were born with a silver spoon in your mouth. If it weren't for people in the hood and projects, you would be out of a job."

The couple standing near the elevator looks at them.

"See, your job requires you to help low income people and provide the services for them. So the next time you try to criticize the less fortunate, think about how your sorry butt is being fed," she said, while getting into the elevator. The couple gets in right behind her.

Gaylin aggressively tries to get into the elevator when the door begins closing. He then runs downstairs and meets CeCe walking by the pool towards the back entrance to the parking lot.

"Don't walk away from me!" Gaylin disrespectfully jerks her hand.

"Get your hands off of me! Go home to your wife! It's three o'clock in the morning and you should be with her!" she shouted, as she hurriedly walks towards the parking lot.

"I'm not finished with you, yet! I'm getting my one hundred and twenty-five-dollar booty call! So take your chicken head back to the room!" Gaylin yelled, pointing towards the hotel.

"I'm not going anywhere with you! If you keep harassing me, I'm going to yell rape! You know a woman like me can accuse a black man of anything and they'll believe it!" She said with shifting eyes.

"You nasty tramp!" He madly shouts, as he forcefully pushes her into the pool. She screams out loud as her body hits the cold chilly water. She falls deeply to the bottom, hitting her head and soon after blood makes its way to the surface. Gaylin shouts to the water in hope that she would hear him.

"I hope you drown, you chicken head!" He walks proudly away without looking back.

Hotel guests heard him, and lights immediately went on in a few rooms near the pool area.

"Oh my God! Harold, there's a body floating in the pool!" A woman shouts out to her husband, while looking out her hotel window.

White flashes of CeCe's limp body floating across the pool kept appearing in Gaylin's sense of thought. He stands still at his front door, holding tightly to the house keys that are in his hands. *Oh My God, what have I done?*

When he walks into his dark chilly home with only a glimpse of moonlight shining through the open blinds, he notices that his wife is fast asleep, slumping over in her wheelchair. He crawls in bed without undressing and deeply listens to the night air breeze whistling across the rooftop.

The next morning, around six thirty, Gail sluggishly awakes with the sound of Jamal's constant cries filling her ears. She then noticed that she had slept the entire night in her unbalanced wheelchair. She looks over at Gaylin who is sleeping peacefully in their king size bed with the scent of raspberry body lotion illuminating around the room.

"Gaylin! Where have you been?!" Gail snaps, yanking the sheets off his covered body. "I sat up all night in this chair! Didn't you care to come home and make sure that I was safely in the bed?"

He rolls over in the bed, glances at her without commenting. Jamal is still crying, in the need of some tender loving care.

"Gaylin! Did you hear me? Where have you been? I was worried sick about you," she said.

Gaylin awakes with sleep still in his eyes and peeps over at the clock that now has seven o'clock.

"Oh my God! I'm almost late for an important business meeting!" He said as he jumps up out of bed and races to the guest bathroom and turns on the shower.

"You still haven't answered my question," Gail mutters as she wheels herself towards the bathroom door. "Where were you on last night?"

The shower is sounding and Gaylin continues to ignore his wife's unanswered questions. Moments later, he rushes out of the steamy bathroom and darts into the bedroom and throws on a pair of blue sweat pants and a gray hoody that are tucked away at the bottom of the closet. Gail has wheeled herself into the living room and is observing the local news, announcing a hotel drowning. Gaylin comes out of the bedroom and places Jamal on his mother's lap and sees the beautiful picture of CeCe, staring back at him from the television screen.

"Honey. Look at the news. There was a hotel drowning not far from where you work," Gail said in disbelief, eyes gazing at the TV.

Gaylin shockingly plops down on the sofa and listens attentively to the breaking news about his secret college lover.

"CeCe Moore, better known as the tattoo stripper, drowned early this morning at The Gardens State Hotel, after she accidentally slipped in while walking too close to the edge." The news reporter said.

"Witnesses stated that she was last seen with a tall black man, around the age of forty. Local authorities have video surveillance of the two checking in the hotel and they are searching for that man for possible questioning. They do not suspect foul play, but an investigation is underway," the news reporter said before Gaylin turned off the television.

"You don't have any business watching bad news all the time." He turns off the TV.

"That poor girl, I feel so sorry for her folks. No parent should have to bury their child," Gail said, rocking her son who is stretched out on her lap.

"That poor girl should have had her butt at home." Gaylin cruelly leans forward while speaking. "There's nothing opened past one o'clock in the morning but a fresh pair of legs."

He kisses his wife on the forehead, grabs his car keys from off the end table and struts out the front door as if he has walked into a new life, full of new beginnings and opportunities. *No pain, no shame,* he thinks happily.

Part 4

You Shall Reap Just What You Sow

Twenty:
Miss Loretta Cox

Dozens of red roses, multicolored balloons and chocolate coated assorted Valentine candy are all being advertised today in flower shops and retail stores, in hope to bring abundant love and affection to all couples on this February 14th. Celebrating Valentine's Day has never been a top priority in Gail's home, because her husband always said he had to work late or had other important tasks on his agenda that never required spending quality time with her. So that day was just another ordinary time in her life where she learned faithfully, through the years, to never rely on someone else to make you happy. Make yourself happy by doing the things you enjoy, regardless if you have to do it alone.

Jamal is nearly three years old and has become a great help to his mother by helping out around the house by putting away his toys after he has finished playing with them, and most of all, he is potty trained. Gail decides to celebrate Valentine's Day at home with her son and watch him happily devour his small box of chocolate candy that her mother had brought over earlier that morning. But her plans to stay home alone are interrupted when Saddie, Nadine and Dion banged on the front door.

"Gail open up! It's your girls!" Saddie shouts from the closed door, holding a flyer in her hand.

Gail wheels herself to the front door and opens it slightly, before the three energetic women race inside without properly being greeted.

"Girl, go get dressed we're going out tonight to the single folk Valentine's Day gathering that is being held at Greater

Monumental Baptist Church in Hollywood Florida!" Saddie said with an upbeat attitude, flashing her announcement.

"Yeah, it's great. I heard that a lot of available good-looking men be there. The pastor will talk about relationships, commitments and how to avoid getting hooked up with the wrong mates in this day in age," Dion said as she takes a seat on the sofa.

Gail wheels herself closer to the women before speaking.

"Have you all forgotten? I'm not single." She said.

"Well, you might as well be. Your no good husband sure acts like it," Saddie sarcastically said. "Where is he now? He should be right here with you, cuddled up in bed whispering sweet things to you."

"He's at work." Gail pitifully responded back, with her head held downward.

"He's always at work. Brother man should have a fat checking account with money falling out his pockets with all those hours he's been putting in," Saddie stated sarcastically.

"Dad not works." Jamal incorrectly speaks while toying on the floor with a stuffed animal.

"Boy, go to your room and play. There's nothing but grown folks in here!" Gail demanded, beckoning him to his bedroom with a finger.

"Child, let that baby talk. He's just telling the truth about his daddy," Dion said in laughter.

"Gail, I think this would be a great program for you to attend. It can help strengthen your marriage and help you to grow closer with your walk with God. I'm not looking for a man, but I want to learn what to look for in a mate when I'm ready to make that commitment," Nadine said, facing her on one of the sofas.

"Well, I'm looking for me a man. A dark chocolate one with big feet," Saddie said with a grin. "He can't be staying at home with his mama. I don't want no mama's boy."

"Amen to that!" Dion said. "I want me a good man, too. All that Roscoe took me through I deserve some happiness. My baby needs a daddy."

"Women, aren't you all forgetting the reason for this program? Pastor Smith is not arranging all of this so that we could grab the next available man after service. He wants us to know the true essence of finding a good mate. It's more to a relationship than physical appearance and money," Nadine said.

"Oh, you forgot the sex." Saddie chuckled, giggling from ear to ear.

"Amen. Don't forget the sex." Dion laughed.

"Ladies, this is serious. You all are acting like a bunch of horny teenage girls. We're not twenty years old anymore and our black men are growing scarce every day. Within the next few years, most of the black men would be either married, in prison, gay, or dating white women. We as black women need to take charge and have some dignity about ourselves," Nadine said seriously.

Saddie and Dion look at one another as they both lean back and stare at Nadine.

"Why do you all think that our black men are slowly choosing other races to marry and bear kids with?"

Saddie looks around the room as if no one is talking to her.

"Huh," Nadine said. "Someone please speak. I'm not talking to myself. Why are our black men slowly choosing other races to marry and bear kids with?" She reiterated.

"Cause they stupid. They don't know a good thing when they see one. Black men think black women are too strong minded and independent. We're not going to be submissive, staying home all day cooking food and washing their nasty feet." Saddie answered with a laugh.

"See there. That kind of thinking done turned some black men away. Men want to feel important and feel like they're the head and not the tail," Nadine said, staring at the women. "A wife should submit to her husband out of reverence for Christ. A husband is head of his wife as Christ is the head of his body and the church. As the church submits to Christ, so do wives submit to their husbands in everything. Wives should serve their husbands breakfast in bed if he wants it."

"If he wants breakfast in bed he should sleep in the kitchen, I'm no one's servant," Dion said with a grin.

"Amen." Saddie claps and waves her hands towards Heaven. "Well, I'm not married and not planning on being married. So I don't give a hoot about the shortage of black men. Heck, they sure did leave behind a lot of snot nose kids in the ghetto and the projects." Saddie vents as she crosses one leg over the other.

"*Bingo!*" Nadine thought.

"Saddie you're right. Fathers who are not stepping up to the plate to be a father to their kids leave behind a lot of children to be raised in single parent homes. See, this program tonight is extremely beneficial.

"I have many students in my class that don't have father figures. Some of them don't even know their daddy's real name. I had one boy to say his daddy name was 'Pat Rat'. I thought 'Rat' was the man's last name. I later found out that 'Pat Rat' was just a nickname," Saddie said, shaking her head in disbelief.

"Well, I've mailed out over five hundred invitations inviting women, all kind of women, to come out tonight to hear this dynamic speech on *Love, Lust, And a Bed Full Of Maggots*," Nadine said. She then reaches inside her purse and hands Gail her cell phone. "Now call your mother to come over and keep Jamal, because this is one event that we're not going to miss."

The night air was cool with drops of rain falling from the sky. The ladies still made their way into the crowded church, with the majority of women standing around waiting to be seated by a few male ushers. The sanctuary was beautifully decorated with red and white ribbons made into a bow attached to the pews. Gail takes a glimpse at the pulpit and sees a very familiar face sitting quietly ready for the service. They both make eye contact and he then waves in her direction. She smiles back and the person comes down and greets her while the guests are still moving abruptly into the building before the services begin.

"Well, hello, stranger," The man said, smiling from ear to ear. Saddie and Dion stare at one another with the *who is this fine man* look.

"Hey, Frank. It's good to see you." Gail said.

"I don't see you that often. Are you still my neighbor?" Frank jokes, smiling at Gail who is glancing at her friends from out the corner of her eye.

"Yeah, I'm still there. I'm busy a lot. With Jamal growing up so fast, I can hardly keep up with him."

"Well, don't be a stranger. Stop by and holler some time. I enjoy your company. Maybe we both can go to Bible study together one evening. That's if your husband doesn't mind," Frank said while flashing a warm smile at her.

Frank walks off and Dion and Saddie eye gazes over at Gail who is still smiling to herself.

"Uh- huh. Who was that?" Dion said with a finger tapping the side of her face.

"He's just a friend."

"That friend sure did look like he had interest in you," Saddie said. "It's time to toss your old dried up husband to the curve and get with that fine piece of meat."

"Ladies, remember why we're here. Let's not forget the focus." Nadine reminded them before everyone took their seats.

Pastor Smith walks onto the pulpit and greets the other ministers, along with Frank, who are all sitting in chairs observing the spirited filled room with people eager to hear what the Lord instructs the pastor to say. While everyone sits attentively with their eyes focused on the speaker, a woman probably around the age of thirty, walks up to the altar with a suitcase and kneels down and prays.

She is extremely thin in size, with unattractive leathery skin and dark penetrating eyes that appear very sullen. She has been living in the city for over a year, and does not associate with anyone. The unusual woman carries around with her a brown suitcase that raises much attention about her sanity. Some of the church members try to befriend her, but her cold and mysterious demeanor shuns many away. However, Nadine takes a great interest in her and they both immediately became church buddies.

"Hey. What she's doing? It's not altar call yet," Saddie whispers in Nadine's ear, looking at the woman at the altar.

"That's Loretta. She always does that. Pay her no attention. That's her way of connecting with the Lord," Nadine replies back softly.

"What's up with the suitcase? She's going somewhere?" Saddie whispered, glancing around the church.

"No, like I said, that's her way of connecting with the Lord," Nadine said quietly.

Saddie continues to stare at the young woman at the altar as she speaks to God silently while the pastor begins his inspirational speech.

"*'Love, Lust, and a Bed Full of Maggots'* is my topic tonight," The pastor said to the congregation as he glances at the big clock in the back of the church.

"I won't keep you long. I know many of you have Valentine dates that you're dying to get home to see, so I'll make it quick and simple for you all."

Saddie smiles to herself and notices that the young lady is still at the altar.

"Why Do Marriages Fail? Marital infidelity is becoming increasingly common in today's society. God designed marriage for a lifetime," The pastor said. "People should be aware of some of the primary causes for marriage meltdowns. One primary reason is that some people married for the wrong reasons. It is sad that some marriages begin for what may be labeled as a 'wrong reason'. I know many of you are probably thinking why is he talking about marriage? I'm not married. I'm here to find out how to get a good mate and then get married. Well, people, you first must know the primary causes for marriage meltdown so that you won't make the same mistakes while searching for a mate."

"Amen," a few ladies in the congregation said.

"Some marriages were entered out of lust and physical beauty. Peter, in the Bible, warns that one ought not to be concerned about the outward beauty that depends on fancy clothes, exotic hairstyles or expensive jewelry. You should be known for the beauty that comes from within, the unfading beauty of a gentle and quiet spirit, which is so precious to God."

"Halleluiah!" the congregation said.

"That is the way the Holy women of old made themselves beautiful. They trusted God and accepted the authority of their husbands. Unlike women today that wears short skirts almost the length of their panties. Some of them allow the men to move in their homes and shack up and then think that he is going to marry them. Ladies, wake up and smell the coffee. If he can have all the white milk for free, he's not going to buy the cow."

"Yeah, that's right. No need to buy the cow," A man said from the congregation.

"People, you're laying butt naked in a bed full of maggots when you allow your body to fornicate in the hot bed of lust."

"Amen," A few folks said.

"Sex is God's gift to married people and sex outside of marriage is foolish. Sexual immorality has no place among Christians. We should know how to respond when temptation comes at us like a stormy wind. God will provide a way of escape from every temptation. Christ can help us, for he, too, has faced temptation. God never tempts people to sin."

Saddie claps her hands in unison with the congregation and notices the young lady is still at the altar.

"Hey. I think something is wrong with that chick." Saddie whispers in Nadine's ear. Nadine is listening attentively to the preacher.

"Sshh. I'm trying to listen." Nadine waves her off.

"Men, you all need to take care of your children," The pastor said. "I'm tired of seeing girls and boys hanging around in the street doing whatever, because they don't have a father figure in the home. If you can lay up all night with the mothers and make a baby, then you can go find a job and take care of them. I'm tired of the government taking my hard earn money out every week just to support your kids while you're off making more."

"Amen. Yeah. Tell it like it is. I get my child support check every month," a young woman shouts.

Saddie continues to gaze at the woman at the altar as the preacher continues to speak. After the services, the lady finally gets off her knees, grabs her suitcase and walks back to her seat. Her eyes are bloodshot red and tears are flowing down her face. Nadine notices the woman crying as they all walk out of the church with the pastor's message still lingering in their spirit.

"Loretta, are you okay?" Nadine asked, her friends walking away.

She looks up at her with teary eyes and speaks through the tears.

"I'm okay. I just have a lot of things on my mind."

"Loretta, would you like for me to take you home? I'm driving my minivan tonight. So I have plenty room," Nadine said.

"Well, I don't want to be a bother. I see you're busy with your friends," She said again between tears.

"Oh, they don't mind. They're good people. Come on, I'll introduce you."

Nadine and Loretta march outside where Gail, Saddie, Dion and Monice are all engaging in conversation. Monice attended the program and wanted the ladies to know she was there. She saunters over wearing a beautiful red dress suit with matching three inch stiletto. Saddie's mouth drops open in shock as she sees Nadine walking towards them with the strange acting lady with the suitcase.

"Guys, I would like for you all to meet Loretta Cox. Loretta is a new member here and she is a very special friend of mine," Nadine said.

"How are you?" Loretta extends one of her hands in greetings to Gail who is sitting in her wheelchair, closer to her.

Saddie disrespectfully folds her hands across her chest to keep the woman from shaking her hands. They all walk towards Nadine's minivan and Loretta holds tightly to her suitcase, mumbling unfamiliar words and smiling to herself.

Twenty- One:
A Woman Scorned

Loretta sits near the window and places her suitcase on the floor right beside Saddie's foot. A foul smell of rotten meat illuminates inside the van. Dion taps Saddie on the shoulder from the back of the van and points down at the suitcase with a frown on her face. Gail, who is sitting upfront, looks over at Nadine who is driving down the street as if the unpleasant odor doesn't affect her senses.

"What's that smell? It smells like a dead rat in here!" Saddie shouts, glancing over at Loretta.

"Oh, sorry, it's just my lunch," Loretta said, partially unzipping the suitcase and grabbing a small brown paper bag full of greasy, tainted hamburgers that the ants were enjoying.

"My goodness, how long have you had that burger packed up? It smells like it was your lunch from last year," Dion said, staring at the strange looking woman.

"Don't worry about it. I'll just stop at the next gas station and Loretta can throw out the sandwich. Let's not make a big deal out of nothing. We all got food in our refrigerator that's old." Nadine interjected, still driving down the highway.

They later arrive at Loretta's country style home, way out from the city limits. It sets off from the road, with a lot of pine trees and bushes blocking the view. Nadine continues to drive down the muddy driveway until the house is visible. When everyone approaches the front door, Loretta escorts the ladies inside with Dion pushing Gail's wheelchair and lifting it up the steps. Inside the house was very dark, with only a plug in night light shining. All of the chairs were covered with white sheets and a black crochet blanket. Saddie walks behind Nadine and coughs in shock when she looks over at the wall that has graphic paintings along with

Bible scriptures. Dion and Gail stare also with a strange look on their face.

"Would anyone like some tea?" Loretta said, as she places her brown suitcase into a closet near the front door.

"Yeah, that would be great," Nadine said while taking a seat on the sofa.

The other ladies' eyes are stun struck glued to the paintings with their hands covering their mouth. A scripture reads: Matthew *5:27-30"Ye Have heard that it was said by them of old time, Thou shalt not commit adultery. But I say unto you, that whosoever looketh on a woman to lust after her committed adultery with her in his heart."*

"Did you all read that?" Saddie looks at Dion and Gail. "Look at those paintings."

In the first disturbing drawing was a young beautiful woman, gouging out a man's eyeballs with a fork. Above the picture reads: *Matthew 5:29" So if your eye--even if it is your good eye--causes you to lust, gouge it out and throw it away. It is better for you to lose one part of your body than for your whole body to be thrown into hell."*

The women let out a gust of air before gazing at the next drawing. Loretta is still in the kitchen, humming gospel songs and making tea. In the second drawing, a man was strapped down on a board, lying flat on his back in a puddle of blood. That same beautiful woman was standing over him with a chain saw cutting both of his hands off. Above that picture reads: *Matthew 5:30 "And if your hand--even if it is your stronger hand-- causes you to sin, cut it off and throw it away. It is better for you to lose one part of your body than for your whole body to be thrown into hell."*

Water begins to sting in Gail's eyes as she holds back the tears in disbelief as she continues to look at the horrifying paintings. *"Poor lady, she's a scorned woman that has misconstrued those Bible verse,"* Gail thought silently.

In the final drawing, a family of three, a young woman and two small children, standing in front of an open grave, weeping and mourning. The grave was opened with a dead man lying in it, with his chest ripped apart. He was holding his bloody heart that was deteriorating with decayed flesh. Above that picture reads: *A stony heart shall not see God.*

"Here's the tea." Loretta comes out of the kitchen holding a pitcher of tea. She places it on the coffee table. "I'll be back with the glasses." She strolls back to the kitchen.

"That chick needs help. She's crazy." Saddie whispers while walking towards the door.

"Wait. She's not crazy." Nadine warmly smiles. I'll explain it to you later."

Loretta comes back into the living room holding four glasses.

"Help yourselves to the tea. I can't drink it all myself."

Nadine makes herself a glass and hands the pitcher to Dion, who is gazing at Saddie and Gail with a *I'm not drinking this mess* look.

"No thank you. I'm trying to watch my weight." Dion lies as she plops down on the sofa.

"I'm not thirsty," Saddie said as she walks away from the door and takes a seat near Dion.

"Oh, I can't drink tea, it gives me headaches." Gail fibbed. *Lord please forgive me for that lie!*

After Nadine and Loretta finished drinking the entire pitcher of tea, the ladies prepared to leave the residence with a great deal of questions for Nadine who apparently has great love for Loretta.

"What's up with that crazy chick? She's has some serious mental issues?" Saddie asks Nadine as the minivan travels from the home.

"She's not crazy. Loretta just needs some love and affection. I've only known her a year and has grown very fond of her," Nadine said.

"Nadine, did you see those drawings? That young woman needs to talk to a psychiatrist. There are people in the world who can help her." Gail speaks from the passenger seat.

"She doesn't need to talk to anyone but the good Lord. Loretta has a chip on her shoulder when it comes to men."

"Really? I wouldn't have guessed that," Saddie sarcastically said. "We know she has a chip on her shoulder when it comes to men. Heck, in all of those paintings she's ripping half of their bodies up."

"That lunatic needs to see a shrink. I've seen cases like that on television. I don't want to be near her again. Don't bring that loony tune back to any of our gatherings," Dion said in disgust.

"Listen to you all! You all call yourselves Christians and you're acting just like the sinner man! I know that Loretta has issues, but I'm not tossing her back to the streets so that she'll become worse! You don't throw away an old pair of shoes just because it doesn't look good beside your other new shoes. You keep them and wear them, too," Nadine said, still driving down the street.

"We're not talking about a pair of shoes. We're talking about Loretta who should be locked up in a crazy house. Even a blind man can see that this woman needs help." Saddie snapped back.

"Yeah, she's nutty as a fruitcake. No one in their right mind would carry around a maggot smelling suitcase full of six-month-old hamburgers. You better get her some help, and I mean fast before home girl explodes," Dion said with a chuckle.

"Nadine, they're right. If you truly love Loretta like you say, then get her some counseling. I'll help you if you want me to. I can feel Loretta's pain. She's a scorned woman who just needs friends like us to lend a helping hand." Gail speaks.

"Friend? That psychopath is no friend of mine." Saddie states with attitude, hands fold across her chest.

Nadine thinks deeply as she drives under the speed limit down the dark highway with fast traffic moving in both directions. She tunes out the harsh remarks that Saddie and Dion are constantly saying about Loretta. She silently mumbles a prayer in hope that it reaches Loretta before any more damage takes place in her mind.

Twenty-Two:
Caught In the Act

Gail finally made her way home as she watches Nadine's minivan drive out of the driveway. The motion light in her yard glowed on the house. She wheels herself into her dark chilling home and realizes that Gaylin forgot to set the security alarm system before going to bed. She closes the door behind her and makes her way into the living room to call her mother. But before she could pick up the telephone, she hears grunting noises coming from the guest bedroom. Her smile instantly fades as she wheels herself closer to the door. Her heart pounds uncontrollably while turning the doorknob. The sexual grunting sounds become more intense as she moves into the room, listening very carefully.

She adjusted her vision and only saw the bare back of her husband moving up and down underneath the sheets. She could swear she heard a familiar voice crying out to her husband as if he is hurting her. Gail suddenly turned on the lights and was greeted with the most shocking surprise ever.

"Oh my God!"

She shouts aloud and Gaylin startling looks back and falls from the bed onto the floor.

"Gail. It's not what you think." He tries to cover up his nakedness with his hand.

"Samantha? Oh my God! Oh my God! I can't believe this!"

Samantha is a fifteen-year-old girl that recently became a member of Gail's church several weeks ago. She is raised in a dysfunctional home where both parents are strung out on drugs and don't seems to care about the welfare of their children. Samantha often stops by the home when Gail needs her the most. However, this particular night, she was unaware that Gail was out with friends celebrating Valentine's Day at church. So Gaylin lured her into the home, knowing cold heartedly what he planned to do to the teenager.

Gail's eyes were full of water as the eyes of the child stare back at her. Gail felt like a transit bus had hit her. She was unable to believe what she had seen and hot flashes began to burn within.

"Samantha, honey, put your clothes on and let's go."

"Mrs. Gail, he made me do it. He made me do it." The girl cries in between words.

Gail closes her eyes and breathes deeply as Gaylin stumbles in the room trying to gather his clothes and explain what happen.

"Baby, hear me out. I came home drunk and I thought it was you in the bed."

The girl begins crying harder, inhaling deeply as the tears rolls down her face.

"Mrs. Gail, he hurt me. He hurt me when I came here to see you. He said if I tell anyone he would kill you and Jamal."

"Gail, baby. That's not true. That little slut is lying! She made her way into my bed when I was laid out drunk! I thought your mother came in and put you to bed!" Gaylin tried to plead.

The fury takes over as Gail tries to maintain her anger. She wheels the chair with all her strength and grabs a picture frame from off their ebony wood furniture and throws it at Gaylin, striking him in the face.

"You pervert! How could you do this to a child? I want you out this house now before I call the cops and have your perverted behind arrested!" Gail said as her blood pressure rises.

"Woman, I'm not going anywhere! I don't know what you think you saw, but your eyes are playing tricks on you," he said, trying to make her feel like she's delusional. "No one in their right mind is going to believe you. I have credibility in this city and I'll have you thrown in a crazy house if you push this issue."

"Samantha, sweetheart, get your clothes," Gail said, with her voice shaking.

"That little freak is a liar. I'm going to have her crackhead parents thrown in jail and she is going to a foster home."

"Mrs. Gail, I don't want to go to a foster home. Please don't tell my daddy or the policeman. I don't want to get a whipping. Please don't say anything." The girl said, balled up in a corner crying.

Gail looked on the floor and saw the girl's school t-shirt, blue pants and pink flower underwear tossed near the bed.

"Samantha, baby. Put on your clothes and we're discussing it later."

The child gathered her belongings and stepped outside the door to give them some privacy. Gaylin stripped the blood spotted sheets from off the bed. Gail made sure he gave eye contact before she spoke.

"You're a low down dirty dog! You will pay for this! If you ever touch another child again, I will kill you! I will kill you!" Gail said with such hate and boldness.

"Whatever," he said with an attitude. "Your threats don't scare me. No one is going to believe your lies and that girl knows what will happen to her if she opens her big mouth."

The room seemed to spin around as Gail wheeled herself out of the house. She later made her way to a payphone and called her mother to pick her up at such a late hour. Samantha sat in the back seat along with Jamal, who was fast asleep not knowing what chaos had entered his home.

"Can you tell me what is going on?" Mrs. Bradford said to her daughter who has dried tear stained on her face.

"Mama, please. I don't feel like talking about it."

"What is Samantha doing with you at this time of the night? Should she be home with her folks?"

"Mama, you know her folks care less what happens to her. Just take us to your house and we're figuring everything out tomorrow."

Gail sits back in the seat and gazes at the moon in the sky. The picture of her husband having sex with a fifteen-year-old girl flashes through her mind. She tried to clear her head, but the images remained, more vividly than before. Tears fell down her cheeks. "Why Lord? Why is this happening to me?" She whispered silently to herself.

Twenty- Three:
A Blast from the Past

A few months later, Gail moved back in the house with her husband for the sake of her son and marriage. She never told anyone what she saw; she is hoping the images would just disappear. But the anger continued to elevate and the flaming torch of hate lingered in her spirit. Samantha was later placed in a loving foster home with people who cared.

It was still early when Gail and her mother began to plan a small Bible study meeting at her home that afternoon. The sun is still bright, shinning gloriously over the land. Monice had previously left her four-month-old son at the residence for a brief moment while she runs around town to do her last minute grocery shopping. Jamal is energetically rolling on the floor playing with the small infant who sits in his baby carriage releasing a toothless smile. Gaylin and a group of rowdy men are in the den, drinking cold beer and competing in a spades game.

"Yeah, I won that hand!" Gaylin shouts as he slams a little joker on the table.

"Not so fast, partner!" Another man said as he throws out a big joker. "Give me that book!"

"Lord, I hope those loud men be gone by the time Bible study starts. Satan got to flee up out of here," Mrs. Bradford said, peeping outside through the blinds.

"They should be here pretty soon. I told everyone to be on time," Gail said with a smile.

"Yeah, baby! See can you beat this!" Gaylin throws out a duce of diamond and gulps down a bottle of beer.

"You got us this time, because I don't have nothing but this seven of heart," one man said as he slams the card on the table.

"Dawg, you still got hearts? You been reneging and cheating over here! Give me those books! You sneaky mother —"

"Gaylin do you hear that?" Another man at the table cut him off. "I hear singing."

Gaylin stops the card game and runs angrily into the living room where Gail, her mother, Nadine, Loretta and a group of women from the church were standing around praising God and singing gospel hymns.

"Hey, you fools got five seconds to get the heck out of my house!" His face is rigid and very furious.

The ladies cease praying and hurriedly gather their things to leave the house. Loretta is near the end table, still kneeling down praying.

"Ladies, where y'all going? We're having prayer meeting. Don't flee 'cause the devil say so," Mrs. Bradford said, racing towards the door to stop the women from leaving.

"I said you fools got five seconds to get to stepping or else it's going to be trouble up in here!" Gaylin warns them.

Gail is timidly wheeling herself away from her angry husband who is shouting and balling a fist up at her mother who is arguing back with her hands on her wide hips. The ladies are standing afar, attempting to leave the house with their purses thrown over their shoulders. Loretta is inattentive still on her knees praying.

"We're not going anywhere. This is my daughter's house, too and she say we stay." Mrs. Bradford flops down on the sofa and opens her Bible. "Have a seat ladies. We have a prayer meeting to finish."

Gaylin madly walks over to Mrs. Bradford and shouts uncontrollably.

"If you don't get your big rump from off my sofa and out my house, I'm going to knock that snuff out of your mouth!"

Jamal runs out of his bedroom and fearfully jumps into his mother's lap. Monice's baby is crying aloud in the next room. A few churchwomen open the door and leave the house. Nadine then taps Loretta on the shoulder, who is still on her knees praying. Mrs. Bradford unhappily grabs her belongings and storms out of the house along with the remaining women, who are walking out the front door shaking their heads in disappointment.

Gaylin notices that Loretta is still on her bony knees praying to God silently without the interruptions of his loud and abusive behavior.

"Get to stepping, too, freak!" Gaylin said to her.

"I'll handle her. We'll be leaving," Nadine said candidly. "Loretta, honey, it's time to go home." She taps her again on the shoulders but Loretta keeps praying.

"I see your girl is hard of hearing," he said as he yanks Loretta up by her sleeve. "Let's get to stepping! Get your junk and get the heck out of my house!" He shoves her into the front door.

Loretta's dark penetrating eyes fix on Gaylin. She stands still for a brief moment until Nadine grabs her hand and attempts to escort her out the door.

"Let's go, Loretta. We're not welcomed here," Nadine said, trying to ease her out the door.

"Yeah, get to stepping," he said. He looks over where Loretta was praying and sees her brown suitcase on the floor. "Take this piece of raggedy garbage with you." Gaylin slings it in her direction.

Gail and Nadine both cover their mouths in shock. Loretta's dark penetrating eyes are now blood shot red. She grits her teeth and lets out a strange grunt as she thinks of the last time someone had put their hands on her and her suitcase.

"Are you hard of hearing, freak! I said get to moving!" Gaylin gets in front of her, pushing his one hundred and ninety pound body frame against her tiny chest.

Loretta suddenly backhanded him in the face as hard as she could. He stumbles over her suitcase and falls to the floor. She then reaches inside of her bra and pulls out a box cutter and insanely runs towards Gaylin, who is partially lying on the floor, touching his nose that is slightly bleeding from the hard blow.

"I'll gut you up like a piece of meat!" She shouts, running toward him with the box cutter.

"No, Loretta! No!" Nadine and Gail holler in unison.

Jamal is crying and hiding his face in fear. The men from the card game stand aside, looking on as if a mad massacre is about to take place. Loretta grins broadly as she places the box cutter to Gaylin's throat. He is shivering in fear, his eyes fixating on the blade.

"You a lucky son of a gun," Loretta said. "I been praying to God to help me deal with my temper and right now, I don't want to upset Him." Her dark penetrating eyes pierce his soul with her gaze.

Loretta closes the box cutter and places it back into her bra. She clutches a firm hold to her suitcase and struts towards the front door and opens it.

"You better watch your back because I sleep with both eyes open. No one gets away with hurting me," Loretta said as she strolls out the swinging front door, with Nadine walking behind her.

Twenty- Four:
Sleeping with the Enemy

Gaylin gets off the floor like a fearful child and peers his head through the window blinds gazing across the lawn as Nadine's minivan rides off. His card game buddies are wiping their foreheads with the back of their hands as their sweat drips incessantly.

"Man, I almost had a heart attack in here. That woman is crazy," one man said, still wiping his face.

"Yeah. I haven't seen a woman that mad since the day my ex-wife caught me cheating with a co-worker," another guy stated. "These women these days are fighting back. There're not taking mess from us anymore."

Gaylin turns around and faces his wife, who is sitting in her wheelchair trying to consume all of the unexpected chaos that has three men shivering in their boots. Her husband, without warning, angrily grabs a tight hold to her shirt collar like a mad man.

"Where do you get off bringing crazy folks in my home?"

Gail is stunned silent, heart racing a mile a minute.

"Huh, answer me, woman! Where do you get off bringing creepy freaks in my house?" He snapped, still holding a firm hold to her collar.

"Gaylin man, chill out. There's been enough excitement for one night." One of the men takes his hand down from around Gail's collar. "Let's go out for a cold beer so you can calm down."

Moments later after Gaylin and his card game crew had left the home, Monice struts into the unlock house and hears her baby crying hysterically in the next room while Gail lays slump over in the wheelchair with her eyes partially opened. Jamal is standing near her, tugging at her beige pants.

"Mama sleep. Mama sleep," Jamal said, looking at Monice. While she inspects Gail's unresponsive body, she shouts, "Gail! Gail!" Monice shakes her. "Gail!"

Monice grabs Gail's arms and pulls her out of the wheelchair and places her flat on the floor. She checks for a pulse and doesn't feel one.

"Oh my God! Oh my God! Let me call 911!"

In the meantime, Gaylin is at a local bar getting drunk from hard liquor and whiskey and conversing with an old classmate about the good old days. His cell phone vibrates in his pocket and he notices that the call is coming from his house.

"Man, I'm not answering that." He turns off the phone and continues his conversation.

"Dude, whatever happened to Peter Smith?" Gaylin said. "I haven't seen that boy since I moved back here from California."

"Peter Smith?" The man questioned. "I don't think I know him."

"Yes you do. You remember gap tooth Peter Smith." Gaylin stated while trying to perk up the man's memory.

"Oh, yeah. Now I remember," the man said. "He died a few years ago."

"What? He died? What happened to him?" Gaylin asked, tossing back a shot of whiskey.

"You know he had that package," the man said while he puffed on a cigar.

"For real, Dawg?" Gaylin said.

"Yeah, you know he caught it from Crystal Robinson," the man said while moving closer to Gaylin. "Yeah, Crystal gave him AIDS."

"Crystal Robinson? Who is that?" Gaylin asked confusedly.

"You know cross-eyed Crystal Robinson," the man said, "Cross-eyed Crystal Robinson that had the clubfoot."

"Oh, yeah, I know her." Gaylin remembered. "She gave him the package?"

"Yeah, man. She sure was ugly, but I heard she sure was good in the bed." The man adds, releasing a smile.

"That's why I wear my protective glove whenever I'm screwing around with anyone besides my wife," Gaylin said as he cuts his eyes at the man. "These nasty heifers these days are AIDS donors, ready to donate it to the next dumb sucker."

"I know what you mean. That's why the Bible speaks on fornication and sexual sins. Ever since I got saved, I've been trying to live right." He looks at Gaylin.

"Yeah, yeah," Gaylin speaks uninterested. "You know church folks are the biggest freaks and we proved that over a twenty dollar bet in high school. I've been suffering the consequences ever since then." He gulps down another glass of alcohol.

"Refresh my memory. I don't recall making a bet."

"Sure you do. You were the one that waved a twenty-dollar bill in our faces betting any one of us to sleep with one of those wall flower church freaks," Gaylin said without hesitation.

"Really?"

"Yes. I won the bet because I screwed that ugly girl named Gail Bradford."

"Oh, yeah, now I remember." He rubs his chin in disappointment. "I sure hate that. I wish I could go back to those days. I was a real jerk back then."

"No need to apologize." Gaylin signals to the bartender for another glass of whiskey. "The damage has already been done. I ended up marrying that ugly behind woman."

"Really?" The man questioned.

"Yes, really. My life has been nothing but a living hell. That woman has brought me nothing but heartache and pain."

"Really?

"Yes, really." Gaylin turns toward him in frustration. "You act like all of this is a surprise to you."

"It is stunningly surprising. Gail Bradford was one of the nicest girls in school. She was a Christian who truly loved the Lord. I can't imagine her being as wicked as you claim." The man sits near Gaylin and watches him intoxicate himself.

"Well, she still does love the Lord. That's about all she loves. She's a pain in the neck and I'm tired of dealing with her. She sits home all day in that wheelchair and reads the Bible and talks on the phone with those gossiping friends."

"Wheelchair? She's sick or something?" The man asked with concern.

"No, that heifer isn't sick. See, a few years ago, I paid my buddy Roscoe Miller a few extra dollars to have this man he knew to tamper with her car so that she could wreck and take herself on out of this world."

The man listens attentively with his head held downward.

"See, that dump fool hired the wrong man because that lunatic wife of mine is still living. Apparently that car accident just left her behind glued to a wheelchair and not the grave," Gaylin said as he gulps down another shot of bourbon.

Monice is performing chest compressions on Gail as Jamal stands aside watching and does not understand what is going on. The paramedics are on the way.

Monice tries to remember how to perform CPR as she tilts Gail's head backward and lifts her chin. She looks into her mouth for food or anything that could obstruct her airways. She squeezes her nostrils as she blows two full breaths into her mouth. She releases her nostrils and watches her chest to see if it rises. She checks for a pulse but doesn't feel one she repeats the steps again and does not see the chest rise, and she can't feel a pulse. She begins full CPR.

"One, two, three, four. breathe Gail!" Monice shouts while compressing Gail's chest. "Five, six, seven, eight, nine, ten, breathe Gail!"

The paramedics storm into the unlocked house with their medical supplies and a stretcher and take over, as the tears rolls down Monice's face. She holds her baby son and comforts Jamal as they both wait for a miracle.

Twenty- Five:
Crime of Passion

Two months have passed since Gail blessedly survived a mild heart attack, which nearly took her life. The doctors said that pinned up stress, anger and a blocked artery was the ultimate cause that triggered the affect. She praises God for keeping his hands tightly around her and protecting her from all harm and danger.

Mrs. Harris, you need to take it easy. Get plenty of rest and stop stressing yourself out. You were lucky this time. She thinks of what the doctor said to her in the hospital room.

Baby, turn your troubles over to God, he'll help you. She remembers what her mother said. *God is capable of handling anything.*

While Gail is mediating on God's grace and mercy and trying to clear her mind of all negativity, the devil comes knocking on her front door, dressed up in tight skinny jeans with high heel stilettos.

"May I help you?" Gail said after she opened the door.

"Where's Gaylin?" The lady said rudely.

"I beg your pardon," Gail said, studying the woman's over made cosmetic face.

"You heard me. I said where is Gaylin?" The lady pressed her lips together, expression very cold.

"Who are you, may I ask?" Gail leans forward in her wheelchair.

"I'm the woman that's been sleeping with your husband and we have a little baby that he needs to be taking care of," she said with a smirk on her face.

There was silence for a brief moment. Gail could feel the pain and pressure rise in her chest as the tears sting her eyes. *Lord not another heart attack. Help me to deal with this heifer,* Gail thinks.

"Well, that's something you have to take up with my husband. I wasn't there when you two were making the baby." Gail closes the door as the stun struck woman stands still on the doorsteps, wishing she had caused a big disturbance.

Gail dolefully wheels herself to her radio and pops in a gospel CD as the tears roll down her unhappy face. She doesn't quite understand why her life has been such a cluttered mess from the first day she became Gaylin's wife. She remembered the choir singing the song "Satan Has Broken Free", a week after her beloved proposed. The song continued to play in her mind until the day she made those wedding vows. *Lord, were you sending me a sign saying don't marry this man?* She ponders.

Bang! Gaylin slams the front door shut and storms over to his wife, who is meditating on the word of God.

"I don't smell any food cooking in here!" What have your lazy butt been doing all day? The house looks nasty with toys all over the floor! You are beginning to be a real pest!" He snapped, scolding her like a disobedient child.

Gail ignores his presence and continues to hum and become busily active in spirit as the gospel music sounds throughout the house.

"Oh, you're trying to play deaf?" He pulls the radio's cord from out of the outlet and angrily shouts in Gail's ear. "Where is my dinner? Take your lazy butt in the kitchen and cook me something to eat!"

Gail suddenly feels the urgent need to spit right in her husband's face and then knock him out with all the strength that is left in her body. But the Holy Spirit intervened and said *I Got Your Back. Let Me Handle This.* The telephone begins ringing and Gaylin excuses himself from his wife. Within ten minutes, he comes back into the living room with a sly grin on his face while he puts his head on Gail's shoulder.

"Baby, I got to step out for a minute. I'm sorry for jumping off on you about dinner," he said. "Is Jamal still at your mother's?"

Gail thinks for a moment and is not going to let him leave the house without first discussing the incident that happened earlier with the young woman.

"Not so fast, buster. A woman came here today and said that you two have a baby," She candidly said.

Gaylin's head rises off her shoulders and he can feel the tension in the air.

"What? Woman you must be crazy. I don't have another child out there." He lied, trying to hide his nervousness.

"Stop all the lies! I'm sick and tired of all the lies! I know you been unfaithful to me and this is not the first time! I've laid in the bed night after night listening to you bring women into our home! I caught you having sex with a child and I never revealed it to anyone! I can't take this anymore! I want a divorce!" Gail demanded, as her voice cracked.

"What? A divorce? Woman you sound crazy! I'm not giving you a divorce until you pay me twenty-three years' worth of my time that I spent wasted on you!" Gaylin looks at her smack dab in the face.

"I can't live like this anymore. You have made my life a living hell and I want out. You can keep the house and all your money. I don't want anything from you except your signature," she said boldly, feeling like tons of bricks have been lifted off her chest.

Gaylin knows that if he gives Gail a divorce, he is no longer entitled to her millions of dollars, unless he gets a lawyer and a request for alimony.

"Yeah, I'll divorce your sorry butt. But I'm getting half of your millions." He gloated, smiling from ear to ear.

"What millions?" *I know he doesn't know about my inheritance,* she thinks.

"You know what millions. Yeah, I know all about that money your dead uncle left you. That's my money, too, because we're married. I'm not letting you leave here filthy rich. You're going to pay me alimony."

Gail opens her mouth and throws up. She cannot believe what she is hearing.

"Yeah, throw up. You're still going to pay me alimony. I guess we're even now," he said with a crooked grin.

Gaylin then struts out the front door with a smirk on his face. He jumps into his sporty Black Corvette and drives off in high speed. Later that evening, around seven o'clock, a slight tap is heard at the back door. Gail disconnects the telephone call with her mother and wheels herself to the backdoor, but first peers her head through the blinds.

"Who is it?" Gail asked loudly.

"A friend of the family, I really need to talk to you," the unannounced person said very apprehensively.

Gail grows quiet and is unsure who the visitor might be this late in the evening. *It's okay. Let him in. This is your one-way ticket to freedom.* The Holy Spirit assures her. She opens the back door and there stands a six-feet-tall, handsome man wearing a button-down designer blue shirt and baggy blue jeans.

"May I help you?" She said, studying his nice dark face.

"Gail Bradford! Boy, it's been a long time!" The man happily said, making his way into the house without being invited.

"Sir, who are you? I don't allow strangers into my house." She speaks with authority.

"Gail Bradford, you remember me?" He walks closer to her.

"Sir, you got one second to get out of my house before I call the police."

"Gail. It me, Clifford, Clifford Williams from Mrs. Bell's tenth-grade science glass," He tries to explain.

"Oh my God, Clifford!" She smiles happily. "I would have never recognized you with the beard. "What brings you here this late in the evening? How did you know that I live here?"

"I ran into your husband at the bar a few months ago and he said that you two were married. I've wanted to come by and speak, but I've been quite so busy." He gazes at her. "You still look great with those cute little dimples."

"Well, thank you. It's been a long time since I've received a compliment," she said with a little distress.

"Gail, I come here today for a reason. I've been holding this back for a few years now. I've been tossing and turning in my sleep because this secret has been terrorizing my soul. Since I got saved, I've been trying to do the right things. I know in high school I was a total jerk, but that's all behind me, now." He pulls out a chair from the kitchen table and sits directly in front of Gail.

"I must be honest with you and let you know what has been going on. I can't live another lie. You must know the truth and the truth shall set you free." Tears sting his cheeks.

The front door to the house opens and Gaylin starts to come in just as Clifford tells Gail what's been burdening his heart for such a long time.

"Gail, I'm so sorry for the pain which I caused. I never meant to hurt you. I was an unsaved man back then and money was my top priority. Do you remember Roscoe Miller?"

"Yes, that's my best friend's dead husband," she said.

"Well, we did some bad things and I'm here to set the record straight," he said as he glares at her. "I'm the one that caused your accident."

Gaylin raced into the kitchen like a mad man.

"What, partner? You did what?" Gaylin said, acting surprised as if he didn't know.

"Good, I'm glad you're here." Clifford said while looking back towards Gaylin. "Now, tell your wife how you and Roscoe conspired that evil scheme to have her killed."

"Oh, God no!" She shouts aloud, grabs her chest.

"Partner, I think it's time for you to get out of here before I put my foot up your rump!" Gaylin demanded, shouting with spit flying from his mouth.

"No, partner, I'm not leaving until the truth is revealed. You were unaware that you hired me to take off those sets of brakes in your wife's car. That what caused the accident," Clifford said, letting off hot steam.

"Man, you crazy! I'll blow your freaking brains out if you don't get out of my house, right now!" Gaylin said, walking towards him with a balled fist.

"Oh, my God! Oh my God! I can't believe this!" The tears are streaming down Gail's face.

"Yeah, Gail. He wanted to collect insurance money and lay up with all kind of women. He is a low down dirty dog. I knew it that night at the bar, talking about how he hates you and sorry he ever married you," Clifford said. "He paid me fifty bucks and I'm here to admit my faults."

Gaylin sucker punches Clifford in the jaw with a balled fist and he falls backward onto the floor, shattering the glass kitchen table. The two men begin tussling around, breaking valuable belongings in the house. Gail wheels herself to the cordless telephone and calls the police. Within five minutes, three cop cars arrive as if a mad massacre has taken place. The chewing tobacco spitting policemen race into the house like a pack of wolves and find the home in unship shape conditions with the two bloody men still pounding at one another.

"Hey, you! You two are under arrest!" One cop shouts as the other two march over to break up the fight.

"Officer, this is my home. "This fool had no right to be here. I want to press charges," Gaylin said, breathing heavily and wiping the sweat and specks of blood from his face with the back of his hand.

"Can someone tell me what is going on?" Mrs. Bradford said as she and Jamal walk into the disorganized home full of cops with nosy neighbors standing on the outside.

"Mama, I want to go home with you. I don't want to be here anymore." Gail cried, grabbing at her mother's waist.

"I want this man arrested. He comes here in my house, filling my wife's head up with a bunch of lies!" Gaylin said.

"You another lie! Officer, this man is a cold-blooded killer. He is the reason his poor wife is in this wheelchair. He should be arrested," Clifford said. "He tried to kill her."

"Oh my Lord!" Mrs. Bradford grabs her chest in shock. "Gail, honey is this true?"

"Everyone settle down. We were called because someone said they heard a disturbance. I need to take a statement from both of you men," one officer said, taking out his pen and note pad from inside his shirt pocket.

"Yes, I'm Gaylin Harris and I want to press charges on this fool."

"Waitttt… a minute. You're who?" The officer looks with a twinkle in his eye.

"I'm Gaylin Harris. Now arrest this nut before I have your badge."

The officers look around at one another with a wide smile upon their faces and then their attention is directly aimed at Gaylin.

"Well, well, Mr. Harris. It seems you will be taking a long trip down the yellow brick road and I mean a very long trip." The cop was very satiric.

The officer takes his handcuffs and places them around Gaylin's wrist. "Gaylin Harris, you have the right to remain silent anything you say can and will be held against you in the court of law. You have the right to an attorney, if you can't afford one, one would be appointed to you."

While the cop continues to read Gaylin his rights, Gail stares up at her mother who is raising her hands towards the heavens in an upbeat mood.

"Every dog sure does get its day," Mrs. Bradford said, waving her hands.

I told you I had your back. The Holy Spirit whispers to Gail's sincere heart.

Twenty-Six:
Deliver Me from Evil

People are overwhelmingly standing around in the street and driveway vigilantly staring in shock as Gaylin is being escorted to jail in handcuffs. He is cursing and mouthing back at the cops while sending a sinister gaze at his soon to be ex-wife.

"No weapon that is formed against thee shall prosper; and every tongue that shall rise against thee in judgment thou shalt condemn. This is the heritage of the servants of the Lord, and their righteousness is of me, saith the Lord." – Isaiah 54:17

"Mama, it's all over. My day of redemption has finally come," Gail said as the police car speeds away with the devil locked down in the back seat.

"Lord thank you, yes, baby. It's all over. Now you can rest in peace knowing that Gaylin Harris can no longer be a threat to you." Mrs. Bradford responded proudly, "Where he's going he's going to need a lot of prayer and God's grace and mercy."

Soon after the excitement outside had come to a halt, Saddie, Dion and Nadine heard on the local news that Gaylin Harris was arrested this afternoon for the December 2002 slaying death of college student CeCe Moore. Apparently, more evidence was gathered on him to pin him as the prime suspect. They had enough fingerprints, witnesses' testimonies, surveillance tapes and letters to go ahead and apprehend him. A warrant for Gaylin's arrest had been issued just a few minutes before someone had phoned in about a domestic disturbance at that address.

"God works in mysterious ways," Nadine said as she walks into the house, where Gail and Mrs. Bradford were drinking lemonade. "Did you all see the news today?"

"No, but I know you heard about Gaylin. Everyone's talking about it," Gail said, smiling to herself.

"Yeah, we heard about it. In fact, we saw it on the news." Saddie replied as she walks into the house, right behind Dion. "God don't like ugly."

"Yeah. I knew that Gaylin was a low down dirty dog, but I never knew he was capable of murder," Dion said. "Wow, God sure does protect us. All of these years we've been living right under Satan's wings."

Gail sadly thinks how she terribly allowed Gaylin all of these years to sabotage her life as if it didn't matter. The signs were there that he meant her no good, but she ignored every call. Therefore, she had to suffer the consequences for disobeying what God had already shown her. There are always things to consider when choosing a lifetime mate. You have to look closely and read the fine print. Everything that glitters isn't gold. A well-wrapped package must be treated the same way as an unkempt one. Everything that looks good to you isn't always good for you. That's how broken marriages, unwed mothers, and numerous sex partners always seem to get the worst end of the stick.

The Bible speaks clearly on wrong doings and His words will never fail. Some people need to evaluate their lives and clean up all the garbage that are holding them back from fulfilling the life that God wants us to have. Stop allowing your body to be used up like an old worn-out sponge and treat it as a Godly temple. Those who wait on the Lord shall inherit his blessings.

"What's wrong, Gail? Are you okay?" Mrs. Bradford speaks.

"Yeah, I was just thinking about a few things," she said, still feeling a bit sorrowful.

"Girl, don't be whining over that scum bag. He didn't mean you any good. I tried to tell you that many years ago.

But you were too much in love with that wavy hair and those sneaky hazel eyes," Dion said, very serious.

"I know. I'm just upset at myself for not listening. Don't you know he's the reason I'm paralyzed, confined to this wheelchair?" Gail heartbrokenly said, eyes full of water.

"What?" Saddie questioned, with her eyes narrowed.

"What are you talking about? How is he responsible?" Nadine asked.

Mrs. Bradford eases out of the armchair and lowers her head as she walks out of the room, very misty eyed.

"He and Roscoe plotted together to have me killed. Gaylin paid an old classmate fifty-dollar just to tamper with my car. That's how I wrecked, faulty brake pads. I almost died. I can't believe that someone could be so cruel. I trusted him. I trusted Roscoe," she said in between tears. "God had my back and I'm still alive."

"Oh, Gail, I'm so sorry," Nadine said, giving her a sisterly hug.

"Roscoe? Roscoe Miller was the mastermind behind all of this?" Saddie said in anger.

"Roscoe? I'm glad I burned his behind up! He's getting his free will in hell and I hope Gaylin is on his way next," Dion said as she looks at Gail.

"Well, I'm free, now. I'm not worried about it. I have forgiven Gaylin and Roscoe. We must forgive others as God has forgiven us." Gail wipes her runny nose with the back of her hand.

Later that night, Lyndia drives one hundred and twenty miles from a boyfriend's home when she receives the news about her father's arrest. Gail, Jamal and her mother are sitting in the den viewing a television show. They appear very joyous with the presence of the Lord flowing.

"Mama, I just got the news about Daddy!" Lyndia shouts as she storms into the house. She walks back into the den and finds everyone in a blissful mood.

"Why are you all sitting around happy like you've just won the lottery? Daddy has been accused of a crime he didn't commit," the girl said, releasing a bit of anger.

"Lyndia, your Daddy is guilty. Everything the news said is the truth, so help me God." Gail tries to explain.

"Shut up! I don't want to hear it! How could you say something like that? He's your husband!" Lyndia acts a little rebellious, swinging her hands up in the air.

"Not anymore. I'm getting a divorce from your father. There are some things that have contributed over the years that you are unaware of. I can't take another minute living underneath your father's wings," Gail said with much content and relaxation.

"A divorce? How could you? Daddy's been there for you and now you want to get rid of him just because he's in jail! You're a hypocrite! He took care of you and nursed your butt back to health when you got in that accident! He was good to you!" Lyndia rattled off like a disobedient child.

"Wait one cotton picking minute!" Mrs. Bradford comes to Gail's defense. "You stop mouthing back at your mama! You know nothing about your father! He's the reason your mama isn't walking! Gaylin Harris has been beating and treating my daughter like a darn dog since the day he married her!"

Lyndia composes herself and stares at her mother in disbelief.

"My daughter loved that man. She done everything she could to hold together that marriage, but he wanted to play around in the street and get women pregnant. Your no good daddy caused my child a lot of heartache and pain. You know nothing about what went on. As a child, you were too busy taking piano lessons and being away from the house. Then when you grew up and went off to college, you were too busy, taking up more time with your educated friends. Where were you when your mother needed you?" Mrs. Bradford said, holding her hands on her hips.

Lyndia gazes with a blank expression.

"Huh, where were you? You hardly came home from college. The only time we ever saw you were once a month or on holidays. If you would have shown a little more love for your mama and came home to visit often, then you would have known that your father was a low down black snake," Mrs. Bradford replied, full of anger.

Lyndia walks over to her mother and gives her a hug and kiss. Tears flow down her round face as if she has lost her best friend.

"Mama, I'm sorry. Please forgive me. I didn't know. I didn't know."

The next morning around eight o'clock, Gail's lawyer comes to the house bright and early with her divorce papers, ready to serve Gaylin. Lyndia has come to accept the fact that her father is a ruthless individual that cares only about himself, but that still doesn't deter her innermost love for him. After Gail signed the divorce papers, Gaylin received his copies within the next business day. However, even between the tiny jail cells, he still has more tricks and evil doings underneath his sleeves. He has a surprise waiting for Gail that is signed, sealed and delivered where she indeed need to start fasting and praying because the devil is still taping on her window.

In September 2003, on the Labor Day holiday, Gail sips on her black coffee in a mug while she eats a sweet cinnamon bun for breakfast. The house is quiet free, with only the sips from her drink is being heard. She meditates on the word of God silently with a song in her spirit. Suddenly out of nowhere, a loud knock is at the front door. She confusedly wheels herself to the front door and there stands her three friends, Saddie, Dion and Nadine, all dressed up, looking very beautiful.

"What brings you all here this morning? Shouldn't you all be out enjoying the Labor Day festivals? Gail said, while allowing the ladies to come inside.

"School is out today and we thought you wanted some company. The baby sitter is keeping my child today. So I'm free to do whatever," Dion said, while walking in the house.

"Yeah, Gail, we thought you wanted some company. It's time to get out and see the world. Stop staying cooped up in this house," Saddie said as she walks in and plops down on the sofa.

Nadine walks in behind the two but appears very gloomy with dark circles around her eyes as if she hasn't slept in days.

"Nadine, are you alright?" Gail said, observing her unusual demeanor.

"Oh, I'll be fine," she softly said voice seems unsure.

"I don't know what's wrong with Nadine. She's been acting crazy for a few days now. She needs to snap out of it," Saddie said.

"Yeah, she was quiet all the way over here. I started to tell her to pull over and let me get the wheel." Dion stated as if Nadine was invisible.

"You two talk like I'm not here. I'm still in the room. I'm just thinking about Loretta. I haven't heard from her or seen her in church lately," Nadine said. "I wonder how she is doing."

"Stop worrying about that nut bag. She's probably off somewhere minding her own business as usual," Saddie said with a laugh.

"That's not funny, Saddie. I care about Loretta just like I care about you all. If one of you were in trouble, I'll be right there at your rescue," Nadine said as she places her face inside her hands.

"I'm sorry, Nadine. Why don't you call her to see how she's doing?" Saddie said with sincerity.

"I tried that, but her phone has been disconnected. I'm worried," Nadine said.

"Well, have you tried going by her house?" Gail said with concern.

Nadine looks up at Gail before speaking.

"No, I haven't. That didn't cross my mind. Would you all like to go to see if she's alright? It would mean a lot to me," Nadine said.

Saddie, Gail, and Dion glance around at each other like a 'I Don't want to go to that house' look. But for the sake of Nadine, they agreed to go, but kept a silent prayer within, because they didn't know what to expect this time.

When they arrived to Loretta's country style home, far off from the city limits, the once manicured lawn was filled with out of control grown weeds and grass, and stubby hedges that were blocking some of the window's view. Unread newspaper scattered on the porch in a pile, mail flooded the mailbox until some of it was falling onto the ground. Eviction notices were pinned to the door and an awful foul smell illuminates the air.

"I got to get inside! She could be dead or sick!" Nadine said as she breaks a window to get into the foul smelling home that leaked urine and feces where the sewage had backed up into the home.

Nadine climbs through the window and unlocks the front door for Saddie. Gail and Dion hold their breath to keep from inhaling the foul smell that is consuming the fresh air. However, when they enter the untidy house, the musty scent of body odor and body waste, sends Saddie gagging in a raging fit.

"It stinks in here! I got to get out this house." Saddie attempts to run out the door, but Nadine's shouts direct her attention back to the reason why they are there.

"Loretta! It's me, Nadine!" Nadine said as she walks around the grimly looking kitchen that has half eaten food in plates where the roaches and rats were feasting.

Dion walks into the bathroom and see feces floating around in a filthy tub of water and used maxi pads thrown in a corner, filled with maggots and ants. Gail wheels herself into an unlocked bedroom and shouts aloud.

"Oh, my God, come here quick!" Gail shouts. Everyone comes storming into the bedroom and gets an eye full that they will never forget.

They enter the bedroom and see an open white casket with a pillow and a blanket inside. Near the casket was a mirror headstone with a comb and a brush beside it. She had funeral home flowers neatly arranged in a row by their colors. Apparently, Loretta used the coffin for a bed and the mirror headstone for a vanity set. Inside the closet there were no clothes hanging, but there was a large black photo album sitting on the shelf that had the statement *"Appearances can be deceiving"* in bold red letters. Nadine picks up the album, opens it and comes across nearly a hundred pictures where all the faces had been cut out. Above every page reads: *"Woe unto you, scribes and Pharisees, hypocrites! For ye are like unto whited sepulchers, which indeed appear beautiful outward, but are within full of dead men's bones, and of all uncleanness. Even so ye also outwardly appear righteous unto men, but within ye are full of hypocrisy and iniquity."* – Matthew 23:27-28

"Oh, my Lord! This is some deep mess," Saddie said as she looks around the room.

"I got to find her!" Nadine said, walking out the bedroom and into another one.

While the ladies were diligently searching the house for any signs and clues of Loretta, her landlord struts in chewing gum and smiling as if the horrible odor doesn't affect his senses.

"I'm here to collect my rent money. Have any of you seen Loretta?" The short chubby man said while glimpsing around.

"Your guess is as good as ours," Saddie said, walking towards him. "My friend, Nadine, hasn't seen that chick in a few months, now."

"Sir, I'm Nadine and I truly need to find Loretta? When did you last see her?" Nadine said, while she walks towards the man.

"She owes me two months in rent. I have already evicted her." He said with a frown.

"Do you have a family member's address or anything that we can use to help find Loretta?" Nadine said with concern.

"Nope. I don't have anything. She said she didn't have family." he replied back, very nonchalant.

"No family? Poor woman, I feel so sorry for her," Gail said.

"Well, if you women happen to run into Miss Loretta Cox, tell her she owes me for rent or I'm going to sue her for my money and she's not getting back her security deposit, because she left this house in a total wreck." The man walks out the front door and doesn't look back.

Two weeks later, Gail is at home enjoying her peaceful time alone with her son. Lyndia came over earlier and introduced her boyfriend, before the two left for the weekend. Monice arrives to the house with a white man dressed up in a blue suit. He is holding a brown envelope in his hand as Monice escorts him to the front door. But before she could ring the doorbell, Gail meets them at the door with a smile.

"What bring you here, Monice?" Gail asked, very kind hearted.

"This is Attorney Griggs. He will be representing Gaylin in this divorce," she said back, with a crooked smile.

"Mrs. Gail Harris. My name is Attorney Randal Griggs. I have some legal forms for you to look over and I would appreciate it if you would agree to the terms so that everyone can get on with their lives," the man said very dryly while handing her a brown envelope.

"Sir, I've already signed the divorce papers. There's nothing else that needs to be settled. I don't want the house and I don't want any of his money. He can have everything. But his money and house aren't doing him any good behind bars. He will never see the daylight again," Gail said.

"You're not God. You don't know how long my cousin will be in jail. They haven't had the trial, yet. So keep your rude comments to yourself," Monice said with a hostile attitude.

Attorney Griggs and Monice leave the premises in such an upbeat mood. Gail has the envelope in her hands and attempts to open it as she closes the door shut. *"Lord what has Gaylin done this time?* She opens the envelope and there are documents stating that Gaylin is seeking alimony and the majority of her assets, including her three million dollar inheritance that her uncle willed to her. The next form is stating that all of her assets, bank accounts, income taxes and everything of value have been seized until further notice. Gail's eyes were stinging from the salt of her tears. She instantly wanted to hurt Gaylin in the worst way, just as he had hurt her. *"Vengeance is mine. I'll handle this,"* her Godly conscious assures her. Gail instantly wipes her face and repented for that bad thought that had entered her mind.

She leaves everything in God's hands as she wheels herself back into the den and reads the Bible to her son.

The next morning the sun is shining so bright and lovely with God's beautiful flying creature, humming a melody tune that brings a smile upon Mrs. Bradford's face as she struts into her daughter's house. Gail appears quite dazed, sitting in her wheelchair with the Bible on her lap.

"What's wrong, sweetheart?" The mother said as she places her purse on the end table.

"Mama, it's Gaylin. It seems like he's up to his old tricks again. I was served with legal papers stating that all of my assets have been seized. My three million dollars that I had been saving to open my own Christian film company has been taken, also. Gaylin is out for blood. He's trying to take everything that God has blessed me with," she said softly.

"No, baby, I was a foot ahead of Gaylin and I've always had been. See, a few years ago, I withdrawn all of your money out the bank and only left fifty dollars in order to keep the account active. Your three million dollars is safe. I took your name off the account years ago. I figured that your deadbeat husband would find out about the inheritance and pull something like this."

Gail stares attentively with a smile on her face.

"The Lord had forewarned me and I listened to his instructions. All of your assets are safe in my name. If they want to seize those fifty dollars, then they can have that because by law, that's all you own. Gaylin can't hurt you anymore. It's over, baby. It's over," the mother said as she hugs her daughter tightly.

"Her Lord said unto her, well done, thou good and faithful servant; thou has been faithful over a few things, I will make thee ruler over many things; enter thou into the joy of the Lord". –Matthew 25:21

Twenty- Seven:
Time Heals Old Wounds

Six months later, Gaylin was sentenced to only four years in prison. His divorce to Gail was finalized and she was able to keep everything, including the house and his sporty black Corvette, because she had clear evidence that he was unfaithful and had conceived a child with another woman. She spends her days praising God, cleaning the house, and raising her son up to be a better man than his father.

Frank, her next-door neighbor, has been away for almost six months in Little Rock, Arkansas, preaching and spreading God's message abroad. However, when he received the devastating news about Gail and how horrible her life had turned out with Gaylin, he soon rushed back to Miami to be by her side.

"Gail, I had to come," Frank said as he walks into the God spirited house with the sound of gospel music playing aloud.

"Frank, it's so good to see you! Where have you been?" She excitedly said, smiling from ear to ear as she closes the door shut.

"Chloe told me everything. I was out in Arkansas, preaching and doing a little evangelism. I had to come. God knows my heart and he knows that you are in a desperate need for a true friend," he said as he takes a seat on the sofa near her.

"Well, thank you. You've always been so kind to me. Yes, Gaylin took me through a lot of changes. He made my life a living hell. But now I'm free. I'm free from underneath the devil's wings," she said with assurance, staring at Frank who is also gazing at her with admiration.

"Gail, from the very first day I laid eyes on you, I was drawn to your inner spirit. I saw something in you that I've never seen in a woman before. You were quite reserved and had that motivation and sincere demeanor that could captivate any man who is searching for a good woman." Frank rests his hand on Gail's wheelchair.

Gail feels a warm feeling erupting in her heart.

"I don't know how in the world you got hooked up with a man like Gaylin Harris. He didn't deserve you and sure didn't know what he had. You're the kind of woman that would make a man want to live right if he's not. You have class about yourself and is a virtuous woman who loves the Lord and believes faithfully in family."

A tear drops from Gail's eyes as she continues to listen to the enamoring words that Frank is expressing from the bottom of his heart.

"Gail, I hope that you don't take this the wrong way, but I love you. I've loved you now for a long time. I couldn't stop thinking about you when I last saw you at the church's Valentine's Day program. I hid my true feelings, concealing what I knew was a sin because you were another man's wife. I repented to God for allowing my flesh to overcome my spirit. He dealt with me in His own way, and that's why I was called out in Arkansas to get away from the temptation that could have brought damnation to my soul." He wipes her tears with the tip of his fingers.

"Don't cry my beloved. I'm here, now. I want you and your kids in my life forever. I want to be the man that can show you great happiness and the one you wake up to every morning. I want to shower your mind with my affection, sensibility and mold your spirit with all the greatness that God has instilled." He moves closer to her and reaches inside his pocket.

"Gail, honey, God don't make mistakes. Sometimes we as people go through life and can't find our purpose for being alive. We walk around every day as if the world has something to offer without first making a sacrifice. Sure enough, we as human beings make mistakes. We choose the wrong mates and could have saved ourselves years of pain, only if we had consulted God first. We as people get caught up in the physical and forget about the inner. There are always consequences for every action, whether good or bad," he said, with his eyes full of water.

Gail's eyes are blood shot read from crying silently. She had never witnessed a man pouring out his soul to her with such gentleness and warmth.

"Sweetheart, I'm not perfect, but I'm working towards perfection with all of God's help. I've made my share of mistakes when I married my first wife. I was a saved man at the time, going to church doing the right things. God forewarned me that this was not the right woman to marry. I got caught up with her beauty and sexy body, where I failed to see the flaws that this lady possessed. She made my life a living hell. Sometimes we as people forget to see the writing on the wall. When you know that's a long black snake on the ground, don't go near it thinking it might be a stick. Trust your gut instincts and allow the Holy Spirit to guide your footsteps." He still has his hands embedded inside his left pocket.

Frank wipes Gail's face again with the tip of his fingers.

"A lifetime commitment like marriage should never be taken lightly. Marriage is not something that should be toyed around with. Some people treat relationships and marriages just like it's a new shirt: when this gets old and worn out, I'll get a new one. When I divorced my wife a very long time ago, I made a promise to God that I would be celibate and the next woman I make love to would be my wife. Some men around my age would think it's ludicrous to sustain from fornication until God sends that special lady." He smiles at Gail.

Gail stares into Frank's beautiful dark eyes and knows that he is Heavenly sent from the most high. Her heart flutters, indicating that God is stirring something up inside that would bring her and Frank a lifetime of happiness.

"Gail, I don't want this moment to slip away. I have something important that I would like to give you and I know that the timing is right. I've already consulted God. He has given me the approval to go ahead and ask you to become my wife. Time waits for no one and I'm ready to start creating sweet memories with you." Frank pulls out of his pocket the most elegant two-karat diamond clustered engagement ring. "Gail Bradford, Do you love me?"

"Yes, I do. I've loved you, too. I've always wished that I could have married you instead of Gaylin, because you have the qualities of a hardworking man who would make a great father and a husband. That day when you gave me and my son a ride home from that busy mall, that showed me that you were a Godly man that has much concern for others. I was impressed with the way you spoke and how you modeled your life after the Bible. I must admit that you are fine as heck, with that shiny bald head and handsome face. I prayed to God to remove those lustful thoughts of you that had consumed my every thought, because I was a married woman," She said with her hand on Frank's thigh.

Frank kneels, his head downward, trying to control the tears that are falling without ceasing.

"See, Frank, I knew that Gaylin wasn't the man for me. I allowed my pride to overcrowd my judgment, because I thought that I had to marry the father of my unborn child. The first mistake that I made was having sex before marriage. If I had saved myself for marriage, then Gaylin wouldn't have been an issue. I didn't want to raise a bastard baby without a husband. Sometimes God allows us to fall deeply into these traps so that a valuable lesson can be learned. I ignored the writings on the wall and went ahead and married a man who I knew wasn't good for me. I fornicated with the devil and ended up awakening to a burning bed of sin." She places Frank's hand close to her bosom.

Frank smiles back at her; his eyes are bloodshot and watery.

"I forgive Gaylin. I can't live my life in torment. I want to make a life with you, forever until the good Lord call's one of us home. I've made mistakes along the way, and now my mind is open to a new beginning and I have God to thank for that. I want to be that special woman in your life who will always respect you, honor you as a man, and always let you be the head of your household as God is the head of the church. I would never think less of you; build up your ego so that you'll be proud to have me around. I'll cherish every moment with you and take every day as another blessing to show my love and commitment because we know not the day the Lord shall call us home," She said as she embraces Frank with a tight passionate hug. Frank takes Gail's left hand slightly.

"Gail Bradford, would you marry me?" Frank said, as he holds the beautiful ring in his hand.

Tears of joy are flowing down Gail's smiling face as she hugs Frank again and replies yes before he slid the ring on her finger.

Jamal has started preschool and is an energetic four-year-old boy who can't seem to ever stop talking. Frank and Gail plan to marry in a few months, surrounded by close family members and friends who are eager to see God's blessing rain down on them from Heaven above.

Every morning just before daybreak, it's always pitch black dark in the bedroom when Mrs. Bradford comes over at the home to get Gail up out of the bed so that she could prepare to dress Jamal for school. Through the years, Gail has become very dependent on her mother and others for help when it comes to her physical incapability, since she's been confined to a wheelchair. This disturbs her a great deal, but she is truly thankful to have people in her life that care about her disability.

Gail meets the preschool bus every morning in front of her house when it arrives for Jamal. She is always there in the evenings when the bus brings him back, but this particular evening, the day the high school kids were celebrating their homecoming game, the bus was late, and Gail had fallen asleep outside in her wheelchair when the bus dropped Jamal off.

The energetic four-year-old boy races toward his mother, who is asleep in her wheelchair, unaware that her only son is home. He is happily waving a note in his hands, extremely eager to show her that he made his first good grade. Suddenly, a strong breeze comes through and the note flies out of his hands into the street. Loud vulgar music is heard from afar along with roaring car engines and laughter from teenagers. The sound grows closer, almost in front of Gail's house. Jamal playfully runs out into the street, very inattentive to his surroundings. A loud car horn blows without desisting and the sound of wheels screaming fills Gail's ears as she awakes from a deep sleep and sees a gray F- 150 Ford pickup truck, almost coming to a screeching halt as Jamal bends over in the middle of the street to retrieve a piece of paper.

"Nooooo!" Gail shouts.

A white light glimpses in her direction as her son's life flashes right before her face. "Jesus take the wheel!" She says to herself as she leaps hastily out of the wheelchair, with sudden inclination and runs hysterically in the pathway of the racing car. As she scurries non-endlessly to save her son, the day of his birth flashes before her eyes. She could feel the throbbing childbirth pain over her entire body as Jamal falls helplessly to the ground as the truck swerves across the street, knocking down mailboxes. Gail picks up her son from off the street and hugs him tightly as she cries aloud. He looks up at her with teary eyes, but is smiling gloriously.

"Mama, that big truck almost got me," he said very innocently.

Frank and a few neighbors, race out of their houses to see what happened. Within that instant moment, Frank notices that Gail is not in her wheelchair and that she is standing tall. But, she is stunned struck and emotional to realize that God has indeed answered her prayers.

"Baby, you're walking!" Frank said as he holds the two in his arms as if he's never held them before.

"Oh, my God, I'm walking!" She looks down at her feet and then takes tiny steps. "I must be dreaming! Pinch me, Frank! Pinch me!"

"No, you're not dreaming, sweetheart. God has answered our prayers," Frank smiles with watery eyes. "We can have peace through prayer."

"Thank you, Lord. Thank you for everything," Gail silently said to herself.

On Christmas Day, December 25, 2004, Gail and Frank Dehner became husband and wife, surrounded by close friends and family members. This was one of Gail's happiest times of her life and for once, she can sleep well at night knowing that she has a God filled man sleeping right beside her.

"Therefore hath the Lord recompensed me according to my righteousness, according to the cleanness of my hands in his eyesight. With the merciful thou wilt show thyself merciful; with an upright man thou wilt show thyself upright."---Psalms 18: 24-25

Twenty- Eight:
It's Payback Time

Gail and Frank have been married now for four years and have a beautiful two-year-old daughter named Jasmine. God had given the couple a wonderful miracle, created through love that will flow on to many generations to come. The Lord made it possible for Gail and Frank to be able to trust again, using their lives as a model to show others that it's not too late to find that special someone if you would just do the right things and sustain from fornication, because there's nothing good will ever come from it. It will just lead to heartache and a sexed up body.

The couple moved away from Florida to a small town in Georgia so that they could raise their children in a rural community without the worries of high crime rates and violence. Gail opened her Christian film company entitled Praise God Productions, which showcases and creates inspirational Christian films that seek to make a difference. Her very first film won an award for the best gospel film of the year. Frank and Gail are partners in the business, and they spend most of their time at home writing scripts for their next award-winning Christian movie.

Jamal is an eight-year-old third-grader who also has a passion for arts. He creates unique looking characters through sketches and drawings that captivate one's heart. Lyndia lives in her mother's house in Miami and plans to reside there in the near future. Mrs. Bradford spends her days visiting the sick and baking sweet potato pies for the churches. Saddie is a professor at the local college in Miami, and Nadine still teaches at the middle school, but she also works part time as a Christian counselor in her new husband's mental health facility. Dion and her sons, live in

Atlanta. She is a print model for the major department stores. Monice is a housewife and a stay at home mother, who works as a travel agency from her home computer.

At least once a year, the friends try to get together and plan something special since everyone's lives have moved in different directions. July 4, 2008 couldn't have come any sooner for Gail who has been counting the days down before her daughter's wedding. Lyndia is marrying her college sweetheart and a wonderful wedding announcement has been printed in the newspapers. She invited everyone to join them in this joyous occasion.

It was three o'clock in the evening; the sky turned gray with the fresh smell of rain in the air when Lyndia prepared to walk down the aisles in the same church, where she was christened. She looked astoundingly beautiful, very immaculate without a stain or blemish to her soft youthful complexion. The sanctuary was decorated gorgeously with royal blue and black ribbons that slightly hung over the edge of each seat.

Gail and her family are sitting on the front pew, along with Lyndia's grandmother, Mrs. Rita Harris, who she has never seen. Mrs. Bradford sits on the next pew, along with Saddie, Dion, Nadine, Monice, and Chloe. Everyone is flashing a bright smile, giving God the praises for uniting this young couple in a modern time where some people would rather live in cohabitation or shack up without a commitment.

Frank, all dressed up in his black tuxedo, stands nervously at the back of the church waiting to walk Lyndia down the aisle. A tall handsome man at the keyboard starts singing a heartfelt melody as Frank gently grabs Lyndia's hand and walks her slowly down the aisle as the guests stand up and face them. The singer's anointed rendition of the song brings tears to many as the cameras flash and the videos tape records to capture this blessed moment that no one will ever forget. What a wonderful time of excellence!

However, within that split second, all hell breaks loose when a big fat white man rushes into the church. He knocks over an usher and there stands behind the huge chubby guy, a man dressed up in a black suit with his hands tucked inside his pockets like a California gangster. His hazel-brown eyes gradually move across the crowded church, in search of someone. The singer instantly stops singing and all the attention is shifted towards the two thugs. Gail makes eye contact with the man and then her heart begins racing and anger erupts. His sneaky eyes catch a glimpse of Lyndia and Frank.

"Well, well. You couldn't wait to jump in the sack with my wife," the man said to Frank, who is holding Lyndia's hand.

"Gaylin! What the heck are you doing here? Get out, now!" Frank shouts, biting down on his lips.

"No, partner, you get out! I'm taking my own daughter down the aisle!" Gaylin yanks Lyndia's arm and attempts to pull her forward. "I didn't get an invitation."

"Stop, Daddy! You're ruining my big day! What are you doing here?" Lyndia said, eyes full of water.

Gail madly storms over to Gaylin like a wild woman and a blow in the face surprises him.

"Oh, the old crippled hank is walking again." He laughs at her. "If you ever touch me again I'm going back to the pen for whupping your—"

"Not this time, man! You will never hurt my wife again!" Frank cut him off in mid-sentence.

The wedding guests are all galvanized, a few of them gathered their belongings and left the church very disgruntled. Lyndia's fiancé shakes his head in disbelief while walking with sharp steps to cease the chaos.

"I want you to leave here, mister or else it will be trouble. The cops are on its way," Lyndia's fiancé said to Gaylin.

"Partner, I have all the right to be here! This is my daughter's wedding!" Gaylin shouts back, shifting his weight from one foot to another.

Gaylin hears the police sirens sounding from afar. He immediately composes himself and releases a crooked smile to Gail whose eyes are red with rage.

"Let me get from around all you church freaks. I'm out on probation and I'm not going back to the pen," he said candidly as he walks near Gail and spits in her face. "That's for backstabbing me, witch!"

Before Frank could sucker punch Gaylin, two police officers enter the church with their guns drawn on the guests. Young children begin crying and holding tight to their parents. The cops overlook the fat white man and Gaylin who are creeping out the front door, as if they're not responsible for the feud. Frank and Lyndia's fiancé explains what happened, but does not press charges, because enough damage has already taken place. The officers leave and the wedding continues, but that joyous moment in history was stolen by the devil himself.

Later that night, Gaylin learns that Gail no longer lives in Miami and she had married Frank and had another child. He goes to a local club and drinks himself a few beers as he plots his next move to terrorize her life. *She's not going to live happily ever after,* he thinks, as he gulps down another glass of beer. While he is evilly trying to come up with a plan to end Gail's wonderful marriage, he sees a drop dead beautiful lady sitting across the table from him. She is stunningly beautiful; her long wavy black hair and pecan brown skin softened her eyes. She was reading the Bible, taking notes after every chapter. He lustfully walks over to her, licking his lips seductively.

"What's up, beautiful?" He said to her as he takes a seat down at the table.

The young woman ignores him and continues reading her Bible.

"What's up, gorgeous?" He said, staring at her cleavage that's exposing her nice smooth skin.

The lady continues reading the Bible and does not look over at him. Gaylin becomes angry and he snaps harshly at her.

"Oh, you're not all that! You need to take your Bible reading butt somewhere else, because this is not the place for church freaks!" He said as he attempts to get up from the table.

The woman's soft brown eyes narrow, releasing a bit of anger, but she hides it with a crooked smile. She composes herself and extends her hand in greetings to Gaylin who is lustfully thinking about sexing her the next minute, as his desires grow stronger. They later leave the club after drinking a number of drinks. Gaylin demands to go home with her, not allowing his good conscious to take control.

Once he arrives to the upscale home in a gated community, the smell of cinnamon illuminates around in the room when he enters the house. The lady closes the front door and walks into the bathroom, leaving Gaylin walking around in a daze. He stares confusedly around the room and feels as though he's been there before. Everything in the home looks so familiar, like a daydream he once had.

The lady comes out of the bathroom, dressed very seductively in a lacy white bra and white thong bikini underwear. She escorts him to the bedroom as she dims the lights down very low. She turns on the radio and slowly undresses him from head to toe and then lays him back on the bed. She crawls on top of him and kisses him as if it is his last. He has an eerie feeling that brings chills down his spine.

Twenty- Nine
You Shall Reap Just What You Sow

Two nearly full wine glasses sit on the end table, as the half- dressed woman hands Gaylin a red rose. He sniffs the flower and smiles back at her as he lays relaxed in the queen-sized bed admiring her irresistible beauty. She crawls back on top of him and passionately caresses his neck and jaw lines with the tip of her tongue.

Soulful music is sounding as she stops kissing instantly and pulls out from underneath the bed a long white extension cord, handcuffs, and a handkerchief. She playfully ties and cuffs his hands tightly to the bedposts and blindfolds his eyes with a white cotton handkerchief. She reaches over on the end table and takes a sip of red wine and fumbles underneath the bed again. She evilly laughs and releases a conniving smile. She strokes his manly chest with her fingertips and then furiously slashes him across the face with a box cutter.

"You crazy witch! You cut me! Get me out of these handcuffs before I beat the crap out of you! Gaylin shouts, moving and trying to free himself from the bedpost.

"Shut up, you piece of trash!" She slashes him again across his face with the box cutter. "When I finish with you, you might not have hands to beat the crap out of no one!"

The young woman tells a story softly as she nurses the wounds in Gaylin's face with alcohol and peroxide.

"I didn't want to hurt you, but you forced me to. See, when I was a child, my classmates at school physically abused me. They tortured and called me names, because I was different. I was raised in an orphanage, never got the chance to meet my real parents. No one ever paid any attention to me until I started having sex. I wasn't beautiful like the other girls my age. I was very skinny, and had skin so bumpy until they called me 'pizza face'. "

Gaylin wails in agony as she dabs alcohol on his slashed face with cotton balls.

"I never got to attend my senior prom, because no one asked me to go. I did meet this boy named Robbie, who said he would take me to the prom if I had sex with him. At the time, I was a virgin, so I decided to have sex with him so that I could go to the prom. My adopted parents bought me a nice dress. I got my hair curled pretty and I waited on Robbie to come pick me up. He never came and I was devastated. The next school day, everyone was standing around my classroom, pointing and laughing at me when I approached the room. Robbie was there also. He walked over to me and spit in my face. The students and some of the teachers laughed. No one came to my defense. I ran all the way home and never returned back to school."

Gaylin moans in pain as she dabs peroxide on the open flesh, eyes still blindfold with the handkerchief that leaks with blood. She then reaches inside her medical bag and pulls out a set of dental pliers.

"When I turned eighteen, my adopted parents said that I was now grown and I had to leave their house and to never come back. I had no money, no family, and nowhere to go, so I slept in the streets, eating out of the garbage cans so that my stomach would stop growling. I then met a man who said that he'd give me a job making a lot of money if I became his girl. I was desperate, wanting someone to love me. I became his girl and he fed my body with drugs for a couple of years. After he finished soliciting my body, he tossed me away like a filthy piece of trash."

She continues to nurse Gaylin's wounds as he cringes in pain. She opens his mouth wide, placing the dental pliers on his top tooth and forcefully pulls it out. Gaylin shouts in agony.

"What are you doing? Please stop!" Gaylin wails, fidgeting in the bed trying to free himself.

The woman continues her story. "I later met a man who was much different. He picked me up from off the streets, took me to his home, cleaned me up and then I became his wife. He was very nice, always showing the utmost love and affection. For once, I was beginning to feel like someone cared. But he was hiding a terrible secret. He flirted around with other women and engaged in unfaithful sexual practices. I heard him night after night on the telephone, talking sexually to women. Many of the ladies I knew. They would come to my house as if I didn't know. Boy, they were stupid, because that's when I went on my first bloodthirsty rampage."

Gaylin shivers in fear as the telephone rings. The lady ignores it.

"One night when my husband was asleep, I pinned his hands down to the bedpost and cut the very thing off that tempted him into temptation, which was his tongue. I cut it off, stitched him back together so that he wouldn't bleed to death, and called the ambulance services. I took that filthy tongue of his and tossed it in my suitcase, reminding me of his terrible sin. I fled the city, nowhere to be found. I changed my name and started anew."

The telephone is constantly ringing as she stitches Gaylin's face together with a sewing needle and thread. She then places the dental pliers on several other teeth in his mouth and forcefully pulls them out, one by one. He shouts out in agony and almost chokes from his own blood.

"I later met another man who became lover of the church. He was a minister who seemed to love everybody. We got married and lived an extravagant lifestyle with nice jewelry, fine clothes and sporty cars. I felt like a princess, thought I had met Mr. Right. But he was also keeping a terrible secret.

He lusted after women with his eyes and could not control his hands. This devastated me, because I was a virtuous woman who truly loved my husband. One day when he was outside, I sneaked up behind him and knocked him unconscious with a broom handle. I strapped his body down tightly to a board, and then I gouged out his eyeballs with a fork and then I cut off both of his hands with a chain saw."

Gaylin shakes uncontrollably as his life flashes before his face.

"I took those dirty hands and those lustful eyeballs and tossed them into my suitcase, reminding me of his filthy sin. I stitched him up to stop the bleeding and called the ambulance services for him. I fled that state to never be found again. My next husband was the one who I had kids with. He was good-looking, but had a heart of stone when it came to making me happy. He was very abusive, beating my flesh to the naked bone. He later naturally died from a sudden heart attack, but after the funeral when everyone had left the graveside, I ripped opened his chest and pulled out his stony heart and placed it in his hands, reminding me that an unclean heart will never enter the kingdom of Heaven. My two kids and me stood around the grave and mourned his death. I couldn't stand to burdened my children any longer, so I left them with a neighbor and fled the state, never to be seen again."

Gaylin shouts out in fear and she slaps him in the face with an opened hand, still pulling out his teeth, one by one, until all thirty-two were lying bloody on the floor.

"I came to Miami about five years ago, trying to get my life back on track. I found this nice church that I attended and prayed non-stop, because I wanted God to forgive me for my sins. I've never killed anyone, but what I done to those Satan suckers were horrifying. I met a nice lady at that church who loved me like a sister. She adored me and I cherished her. She was my only friend and I miss her dearly. But what troubled me was her friend who was in the wheelchair."

Gaylin swallowed hard and his heart began racing a mile a minute, blood slowly dripped as she stitched his face.

"Her friend in the wheelchair was so sweet and God filled. She was married to an egotistical man who despised the ground she walked. He was ruthless, just like the men from my past. I felt sorry for her that day when he angrily threw me out the house. I told him that his day of reaping would come, sooner than he expected. If you don't know by now, my name is Miss Loretta Cox, that crazy looking woman with the brown suitcase that you madly bounced out your house, because you didn't want your wife to have Bible study, something she truly enjoys."

Gaylin breathed deeply as the sweat drips down his wounded face and excruciating pain coming from his mouth.

"I carry around that brown suitcase, full of disgusting tainted fleshly sin, to remind me of what I done."

She places the box cutter between Gaylin's legs and he lets out a loud cry.

"Please, Loretta, don't do this." He pleads in between cries.

"Shut up, you Satan son of a gun! I'll stop when I'm finished!" She shouts back, growing angrier.

She lifts Gaylin's manhood, as it stands stiff, very erect. She parades the blade around it, teasing him dearly.

"Oh, God, please help me!" Gaylin yells out for mercy.

"Shut up, you scum bag! You never called on Jesus before! You should have served Him a long time ago! Don't wait until you get in trouble to call on Him, because he might not answer! You had all these chances to turn your life around, but you didn't! You chose to serve the devil, always calling Christians 'church freaks'!"

Gaylin shivers in fear before speaking, "I'm sorry! Please don't do this!"

"It's too late for apologies! You didn't apologize to your poor wife when you paid that man fifty-dollars to tamper with her car that caused her to be paralyzed! You never apologized for beating the crap out of her when you knew that she was helpless, confined to a wheelchair! You never apologized for bringing strange women to her house and sexed them right next door while she slept! You never apologized for impregnating another woman and lying about it! You never apologized for molesting that young girl! And most of all, you never apologized to God!"

Gaylin lets out a gust of air as the tears sting his swollen aching face and mouth. Loretta madly flips him onto his stomach and she reaches into her medical purse and pulls out a white plastic bag full of brown railroad rocks. She insanely thrusts the railroad rocks, one by one, up Gaylin's rectum, splitting his anus tissues as blood splatters.

"Oooh! My God! My Lord and Savior Jesus Christ, please help me!" He lets out a loud painful cry as his body begins to swell.

"Shut up! Shut up right now or I'm going to stuff your mouth with your own nuts!" She shouts like she's crazy as a bedbug.

Loretta again reaches inside her medical bag and retrieves the most powerful glue in the world. She glues Gaylin's butt cheeks together, gluing it so tightly that the glue cannot be easily dissolved. Next, with her bare hands, she gouges out his hazel-brown eyes that he adores so much and then stitches his eye socket shut.

The anguish cry of Gaylin goes through the open window, and lingers in the night air. It is a painful and airy sound that awakes the peacefully sleeping neighbors. Gaylin instantly remembers that this very moment was a dream that he had previously had that is now a reality. Although he didn't serve God, God still loved him and had forewarned him in a dream what would soon happen to him if he didn't change his evil lifestyle.

Loretta stitches him back together to stop the bleeding and tosses his bloody eyeballs inside her brown suitcase. The pain is so excruciating, his tears refuse to fall. He shivers and wails in pain as if he's having spasm. She goes into the bathroom and washes herself up. She puts on a nice dark colored outfit before calling the ambulance services for Gaylin; leaving a note pinned to the front door that reads: *"It's over now. My work has been done. God will forgive my sins if I willingly confess them. Repentance of sin opens the way for a relationship with God."*

Miss Loretta Cox walks happily off her porch, carrying her brown suitcase in her hand. *"Weeping May endureth for a night, but joy comes in the morning.*

She smiles and thinks as she struts down the quiet dark road never to be seen again.

About The Author

Melissa Diane Hudson has a Master's degree in Education and a Bachelor of Arts degree in psychology. She is a 2012 Georgia author awards nominee for her relationship book *The Female Fool: 10 Reasons Why You Aren't Attracting a Good Christian Man.* She has appeared on various radio talk shows across America, and was a guest on national television talk show *The Montel Williams Show.* Ms. Hudson was featured in an International Women magazine entitled *Woman.* She is a widow and lives in Albany, Georgia with her son.

235

Midnight Creeping, Early Morning Reaping

238

www.ingramcontent.com/pod-product-compliance
Lightning Source LLC
Chambersburg PA
CBHW070444120726
47910CB00003B/923